THE FIRST LAW OF ROBOTICS:

"A robot may not injure a human being, or, through inaction, allow a human being to come to harm."

So how could Robot MA-2 abandon its owner to certain death?
How could Robot LNE-Pr break its master's arm with a blow of its fist?
How could Robot EZ-27 turn against its owner and utterly ruin him?

Meet Dr. Susan Calvin, robopsychologist, whose mission is to investigate the robots and save humanity from destruction at their hands!

ISAAC ASIMOV

EIGHT STORIES FROM THE REST OF THE ROBOTS

BERKLEY BOOKS, NEW YORK

This Berkley book contains the complete text of the original hardcover edition. It has been completely reset in a typeface designed for easy reading, and was printed from new film.

EIGHT STORIES FROM THE REST OF THE ROBOTS

A Berkley Book / published by arrangement with Doubleday & Company, Inc.

PRINTING HISTORY
Doubleday edition published 1964
Jove edition / March 1978
Berkley edition / August 1983

A BERKLEY BOOK ® TM 757,375
Berkley Books are published by The Berkley Publishing Group, 200 Madison Avenue, New York, New York 10016.
The name "BERKLEY" and the stylized "B" with design are trademarks belonging to Berkley Publishing Corporation.
PRINTED IN THE UNITED STATES OF AMERICA

To Tim, Tom and Dick
my stalwart supporters at Doubleday

Contents

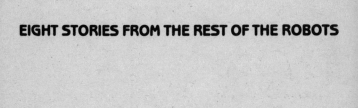

EIGHT STORIES FROM THE REST OF THE ROBOTS

Introduction

Would you like to hear a writer's nightmare?

Well, then, imagine a writer of considerable reputation, who knows himself to be a Great Man. Bestow upon him a wife, a little woman who is a bit of a writer herself but, of course, nothing like her great, her magnificent husband, either in her own eyes, in the world's eyes, or (most important of all) in his eyes.

And imagine that, as a result of some conversation, the little woman suggests she write a novel on the subject. And the Great Man, smiling benignly, says, "Of course, dear. You go right ahead."

And she does, and it is published, and it makes a perfectly gigantic sensation. And it follows, then, that although the Great Man is universally admitted to be Great, it is the little woman's novel which is best known forever atferward—so well known, in fact, that the title becomes a byword in the English language.

How grisly a situation for a normally egocentric professional writer that would be.

1

Yet I'm not making this up. It is a true story. It happened.

The Great Man is Percy Bysshe Shelley, one of the magnificent lyric poets of the English language. At the age of twenty-two, he eloped with Mary Wollstonecraft Godwin, an event which, however romantic, was slightly irregular, as Shelley was a married man at the time.

The publicity was such that they were better off outside England, and in the summer of 1816 they stayed on the shores of Lake Geneva in Switzerland with the equally great poet and equally notorious gentleman, George Gordon, Lord Byron.

At the time, the scientific world was in a ferment. In 1791 the Italian physicist, Luigi Galvani, had discovered that frogs' muscles could be made to twitch if touched simultaneously by two different metals and it seemed to him that living tissue was filled with "animal electricity." This theory was disputed by another Italian physicist, Alessandro Volta, who showed that electric currents could be produced by the juxtaposition of different metals without the presence of living or once-living tissue. Volta had invented the first battery and the English chemist, Humphry Davy, went on in 1807 and 1808 to build an unprecedentedly powerful one and to carry out, with its help, all sorts of chemical reactions that had been impossible to chemists of the non-electrical age.

Electricity was therefore a word of power and, although Galvani's "animal electricity" had been quickly smashed by the researches of Volta, it remained a magic phrase among the lay public. Interest in the relationship of electricity to life was intense.

One evening a small group including Byron, Shelley, and Mary Godwin discussed the possibility of actually creating life by means of electricity, and it occurred to Mary that she might write a fantasy on the subject. Byron and Shelley approved; in fact they thought they, too, might write fantastic novels for the private amusement of the little company.

Only Mary actually carried this through. At the end of the year the first Mrs. Shelley committed suicide, so that Shelley and Mary could marry and return to England. In England, in 1817, Mary Shelley's novel was completed and in 1818 it was published. It was about a young scientist, a student of anatomy, who assembled a being in his laboratory and succeeded in infusing it with life by way of electricity. The being (given no name) was a monstrous eight-foot creature with a horrible face that frightened all beholders into fits.

The monster can find no place in human society and, in his misery, turns upon the scientist and all those dear to him. One by one the scientist's relatives (including his bride) are destroyed and in the end the scientist dies as well. The monster wanders off into the wilderness, presumably to die of remorse.

The novel made a huge sensation and has never stopped making a huge sensation. There is simply no question as to which Shelley made the greater mark on people generally. To the students of literature, the Shelley may be Percy Bysshe, of course, but stop people on the street and ask them if they've ever heard of Adonais, or Ode to the West Wind, or The Cenci. Maybe they have, but very likely they have not. Then ask them if they have ever heard of Frankenstein.

For Frankenstein was the name of Mrs. Shelley's novel and of the young scientist who created the monster. Ever since, "a Frankenstein" has been used for anyone or anything that creates something that destroys the creator. The exclamation "I have created a Frankenstein's monster" has become such a cliché that it can be used only humorously nowadays.

Frankenstein achieved its success, at least in part, because it was a restatement of one of the enduring fears of mankind—that of dangerous knowledge. Frankenstein was another Faust, seeking knowledge not meant for man, and he had created his Mephistophelean nemesis.

In the early nineteenth century the exact nature of Frankenstein's sacrilegious invasion of forbidden knowledge was clear. Man's advancing science might, conceivably, imbue dead matter with life; but nothing man could do could create a soul, for that was God's exclusive domain. Frankenstein therefore could, at best, create a soulless intelligence, and such an ambition was evil and deserving of ultimate punishment.

The theological "thou shalt not" barrier against man's

advancing knowledge and intensifying science weakened as the nineteenth century progressed. The industrial revolution broadened and deepened and the Faustian motif gave way, temporarily, to a buoyant belief in progress and an inevitably approaching utopia-through-science.

This dream, alas, was shattered by World War I. That horrible holocaust made it quite plain that science could, after all, be an enemy of humanity. It was through science that new explosives were manufactured and that airplanes and airships were constructed to carry those explosives to areas behind the lines that earlier might have been secure. It was science that made possible, in particular, that ultimate horror of the trenches, poison gas.*

Consequently the Evil Scientist or, at best, the Foolishly Sacrilegious Scientist became a stock character in post-World War I science fiction.

In the days immediately following the war an extremely dramatic and influential example of this motif was advanced, again revolving about the creation of quasi-life. This was the play R.U.R. by the Czech writer, Karel Capek. It was written in 1921 and translated into English in 1923. R.U.R. stood for Rossum's Universal Robots. Like Frankenstein, Rossum had discovered the secret of creating artificial men. These were called "robots" from a Czech word meaning "worker," and the word entered the English language and gained a strong hold there.

The robots were intended, as their name implies, to be workers, but all goes wrong. Mankind, its motivation lost, ceases to reproduce itself. Statesmen learn to use the robots in war. The robots themselves rise in rebellion, destroy what is left of mankind and take over the world.

Once again the scientific Faust has been destroyed by his Mephisophelean creation.

In the 1920s science fiction was becoming a popular art form for the first time, and no longer merely a tour de

---

*The Faustian role of science in World War I was dwarfed to insignificance by its role in World War II and in the Cold War. The hydrogen bomb and bacteriological warfare reduce poison-gas attacks to mere inconveniences.

force in the hands of an occasional master such as Verne and Wells. Magazines devoted exclusively to science fiction appeared and "science fiction writers" made their appearance on the literary scene.

And one of the stock plots of science fiction was that of the invention of a robot—usually pictured as a creature of metal, without soul or emotion. Under the influence of the well-known deeds and ultimate fate of Frankenstein and Rossum, there seemed only one change to be rung on this plot.—Robots were created and destroyed their creator; robots were created and destroyed their creator; robots were created and destroyed their creator—

In the 1930s I became a science-fiction reader, and I quickly grew tired of this dull hundred-times-told tale. As a person interested in science, I resented the purely Faustian interpretation of science.

Knowledge has its dangers, yes, but is the response to be a retreat from knowledge? Are we prepared then to return to the ape and forfeit the very essence of humanity? Or is knowledge to be used as itself a barrier against the danger it brings?

In other words, Faust must indeed face Mephistopheles, but Faust does not have to be defeated!

Knives are manufactured with hilts so that they may be grasped safely, stairs possess banisters, electric wiring is insulated, pressure cookers have safety valves—in every artifact, thought is put into minimizing danger. Sometimes the safety achieved is insufficient because of limitations imposed by the nature of the universe or the nature of the human mind. However, the effort is there.

Consider a robot, then, as simply another artifact. It is not a sacrilegious invasion of the domain of the Almighty, any more (or any less) than any other artifact is. As a machine, a robot will surely be designed for safety, as far as possible. If robots are so advanced that they can mimic the thought processes of human beings, then surely the nature of those thought processes will be designed by human engineers and built-in safeguards will be added. The safety may not be perfect (what is?), but it will be as complete as men can make it.

With all this in mind I began, in 1940, to write robot

stories of my own—but robot stories of a new variety. Never, never, was one of my robots to turn stupidly on his creator for no purpose but to demonstrate, for one more weary time, the crime and punishment of Faust.

Nonsense! My robots were machines designed by engineers, not pseudo-men created by blasphemers. My robots reacted along the rational lines that existed in their "brains" from the moment of construction.

I must admit, though, that occasionally, in my early attempts, I saw the robot as little more than a figure of fun. I pictured it as a completely harmless creature, intent only on doing the work for which it was designed. It was incapable of harming men, yet it was victimized by human beings who, suffering from a "Frankenstein complex" (as I called it in some of my stories), insisted on considering the poor machines to be deadly dangerous creatures.

An example of this is "Robot AL-76 Goes Astray," which first appeared in the February, 1942, Amazing Stories.

PART I

The Coming of the Robots

Robot AL-76 Goes Astray

Jonathan Quell's eyes crinkled worriedly behind their rimless glasses as he charged through the door labeled "General Manager."

He slapped the folded paper in his hands upon the desk and panted, "Look at that, boss!"

Sam Tobe juggled the cigar in his mouth from one cheek to the other, and looked. His hand went to his unshaven jaw and rasped along it. "Hell!" he exploded. "What are they talking about?"

"They say we sent out five AL robots," Quell explained, quite unnecessarily.

"We sent six," said Tobe.

"Sure, six! But they only got five at the other end. They sent out the serial numbers and AL-76 is missing."

Tobe's chair went over backward as he heaved his thick bulk upright and went through the door as if he were on greased wheels. It was five hours after that—with the plant pulled apart from assembly rooms to vacuum chambers; with every one of the plant's two hundred employees put through the third-degree mill—that a sweating, disheveled Tobe sent an emergency message to the central plant at Schenectady.

And at the central plant, a sudden explosion of near panic took place. For the first time in the history of the United States Robots and Mechanical Men Corporation, a robot had escaped to the outer world. It wasn't so much that the law forbade the presence of any robot on Earth outside a licensed factory of the corporation. Laws could always be squared. What was much more to the point was the statement made by one of the research mathematicians.

He said: "That robot was created to run a Disinto on the moon. Its positronic brain was equipped for a lunar environment, and *only* a lunar environment. On Earth it's going to receive seventy-five umptillion sense impressions for which it was never prepared. There's no telling *what* its reactions will be. No telling!" And he wiped a forehead that had suddenly gone wet, with the back of his hand.

Within the hour a stratoplane had left for the Virginia plant. The instructions were simple.

"Get that robot, and get it fast!"

AL-76 was confused! In fact, confusion was the only impression his delicate positronic brain retained. It had started when he had found himself in these strange surroundings. How it had come about, he no longer knew. Everything was mixed up.

There was green underfoot, and brown shafts rose all about him with more green on top. And the sky was blue where it should have been black. The sun was all right, round and yellow and hot—but where was the powdery pumice rock underfoot; where were the huge clifflike crater rings?

There was only the green below and the blue above. The sounds that surrounded him were all strange. It was blue and cold and wet. And when he passed people, as he did, occasionally, they were without the space suits they should have been wearing. When they saw him, they shouted and ran.

One man had leveled a gun at him and the bullet had whistled past his head—and then that man had run too.

He had no idea of how long he had been wandering before he finally stumbled upon Randolph Payne's shack two miles out in the woods from the town of Hannaford. Randolph Payne himself—a screwdriver in one hand, a pipe in the other and a battered ruin of a vacuum cleaner between his knees—squatted outside the doorway.

Payne was humming at the time, for he was a naturally happy-go-lucky soul—when at his shack. He had a more respectable dwelling place back in Hannaford, but *that* dwelling place was pretty largely occupied by his wife, a fact which he silently but sincerely regretted. Perhaps, then, there was a sense of relief and freedom at such times as he found himself able to retire to his "special deluxe doghouse" where he could smoke in peace and attend to his hobby of reservicing household appliances.

It wasn't much of a hobby, but sometimes someone would bring out a radio or an alarm clock and the money he would get paid for juggling its insides was the only money he ever got that didn't pass in driblets through his spouse's niggardly hands.

This vacuum cleaner, for instance, would bring in an easy six bits.

At the thought he broke into song, raised his eyes, and broke into a sweat. The song choked off, the eyes popped, and the sweat became more intense. He tried to stand up—as a preliminary to running like hell—but he couldn't get his legs to cooperate.

And then AL-76 had squatted down next to him and said, "Say, why did all the rest of them run?"

Payne knew quite well why they all ran, but the gurgle that issued from his diaphragm didn't show it. He tried to inch away from the robot.

AL-76 continued in an aggrieved tone, "One of them even took a shot at me. An inch lower and he would have scratched my shoulder plate."

"M-must have b-been a nut," stammered Payne.

"That's possible." The robot's voice grew more confidential. "Listen, what's wrong with everything?"

Payne looked hurriedly about. It had struck him that the robot spoke in a remarkably mild tone for one so heavily and brutally metallic in appearance. It also struck him that he had heard somewhere that robots were mentally incapable of harming human beings. He relaxed a bit.

"There's nothing wrong with anything."

"Isn't there?" AL-76 eyed him accusingly. *"You're* all wrong. Where's your space suit?"

"I haven't got any."

"Then why aren't you dead?"

That stopped Payne, "Well—I don't know."

"See!" said the robot triumphantly, "there's something wrong with everything. Where's Mount Copernicus? Where's Lunar Station 17? And where's my Disinto? I want to get to work, I do." He seemed perturbed, and his voice shook as he continued. "I've been going about for hours trying to get someone to tell me where my Disinto is, but they all run away. By now I'm probably 'way behind schedule and the Sectional Executive will be as sore as blazes. This is a fine situation."

Slowly Payne unscrambled the stew in which his brain found itself and said, "Listen, what do they call you?"

"My serial number is AL-76."

"All right, Al is good enough for me. Now, Al, if you're looking for Lunar Station 17, that's on the moon, see?"

AL-76 nodded his head ponderously. "Sure. But I've been looking for it—"

"But it's on the moon. This isn't the moon."

It was the robot's turn to become confused. He watched Payne for a speculative moment and then said slowly, "What do you mean this isn't the moon? Of course it's the moon. Because if it isn't the moon, what is it, huh? Answer me that."

Payne made a funny sound in his throat and breathed hard. He pointed a finger at the robot and shook it. "Look," he said— and then the brilliant idea of the century struck him, and he finished with a strangled "Wow!"

AL-76 eyed him censoriously. "That isn't an answer. I think I have a right to a civil answer if I ask a civil question."

Payne wasn't listening. He was still marveling at himself. Why, it was as plain as day. This robot was one built for the moon that had somehow gotten loose on Earth. Naturally it would be all mixed up, because its positronic brain had been geared exclusively for a lunar environment, making its earthly surroundings entirely meaningless.

And now if he could only keep the robot here—until he could get in touch with the men at the factory in Petersboro. Why, robots were worth money. The cheapest cost $50,000, he had once heard, and some of them ran into millions. Think of the reward!

Man, oh, man, *think of the reward!* And every cent for himself. Not as much as a quarter of a snifter of a plugged nickel for Mirandy. Jumpin' tootin' blazes, *no!*

He rose to his feet at last. "Al," he said, "you and I are buddies! Pals! I love you like a brother." He thrust out a hand. "Shake!"

The robot swallowed up the offered hand in a metal paw and squeezed it gently. He didn't quite understand. "Does that mean you'll tell me how to get to Lunar Station 17?"

Payne was a trifle disconcerted. "N-no, not exactly. As a matter of fact, I like you so much, I want you to stay here with me awhile."

"Oh no, I can't do that. I've got to get to work." He shook his head. "How would you like to be falling behind your quota hour by hour and minute by minute? I want to work. I've *got* to work."

Payne thought sourly that there was no accounting for tastes, and said, "All right, then, I'll explain something to you — because I can see from the looks of you that you're an intelligent person. I've had orders from your Sectional Executive, and he wants me to keep you here for a while. Till he sends for you, in fact."

"What for?" asked AL-76 suspiciously.

"I can't say. It's secret government stuff." Payne prayed, inwardly and fervently, that the robot would swallow this. Some robots were clever, he knew, but this looked like one of the early models.

While Payne prayed, AL-76 considered. The robot's brain, adjusted to the handling of a Disinto on the moon, was not at its best when engaged in abstract thought, but just the same, ever since he had gotten lost, AL-76 had found his thought processes becoming stranger. The alien surroundings did something to him.

His next remark was almost shrewd. He said slyly, "What's my Sectional Executive's name?"

Payne gulped and thought rapidly. "Al," he said in a pained fashion, "you hurt me with this suspicion. I *can't* tell you his name. The trees have ears."

AL-76 inspected the tree next to him stolidly and said, "They have not."

"I know. What I mean is that spies are all around."

"Spies?"

"Yes. You know, *bad* people who want to destroy Lunar Station 17."

"What for?"

"Because they're *bad*. And they want to destroy *you*, and that's why you've got to stay here for a while, so they can't find you."

"But—but I've got to have a Disinto. I mustn't fall behind my quota."

"You will have. You will have," Payne promised earnestly, and just as earnestly damned the robot's one-track mind. "They're going to send one out tomorrow. Yeah, tomorrow." That would leave plenty of time to get the men from the factory out here and collect beautiful green heaps of hundred-dollar bills.

But AL-76 grew only the more stubborn under the distressing impingement of the strange world all about him upon his thinking mechanism.

"No," he said, "I've got to have a Disinto now." Stiffly he straightened his joints, jerking erect. "I'd better look for it some more."

Payne swarmed after and grabbed a cold, hard elbow. "Listen," he squealed, "You've got to stay—"

And something in the robot's mind clicked. All the strangeness surrounding him collected itself into one globule, exploded, and left a brain ticking with a curiously increased efficiency. He whirled on Payne. "I tell you what. I can build a Disinto right here—and then I can work it."

Payne paused doubtfully. "I don't think I can build one." He wondered if it would do any good to pretend he could.

"That's all right." AL-76 could almost feel the positronic paths of his brain weaving into a new pattern, and experienced a strange exhilaration. "I can build one." He looked into Payne's deluxe doghouse and said, "You've got all the material here that I need."

Randolph Payne surveyed the junk with which his shack was filled: eviscerated radios, a topless refrigerator, rusty automobile engines, a broken-down gas range, several miles of frayed wire, and, taking it all together, fifty tons or thereabouts of the most heterogeneous mass of old metal as ever caused a junkman to sniff disdainfully.

"Have I?" he said weakly.

• • •

Two hours later, two things happened practically simultaneously. The first was that Sam Tobe of the Petersboro branch of the United States Robot and Mechanical Men Corporation received a visiphone call from one Randolph Payne of Hannaford. It concerned the missing robot, and Tobe, with a deep-throated snarl, broke connection halfway through and ordered all subsequent calls to be rerouted to the sixth assistant vice-president in charge of buttonholes.

This was not really unreasonable of Tobe. During the past week, although Robot AL-76 had dropped from sight completely, reports had flooded in from all over the Union as to the robot's whereabouts. As many as fourteen a day came—usually from fourteen different states.

Tobe was almighty tired of it, to say nothing of being half crazy on general principles. There was even talk of a Congressional investigation, though every reputable roboticist and mathematical physicist on Earth swore the robot was harmless.

In his state of mind, then, it is not surprising that it took three hours for the general manager to pause and consider just exactly how it was that this Randolph Payne had known that the robot was slated for Lunar Station 17, and, for that matter, how he had known that the robot's serial number was AL-76. Those details had not been given out by the company.

He kept on considering for about a minute and a half and then swung into action.

However, during the three hours between the call and the action, the second event took place. Randolph Payne, having correctly diagnosed the abrupt break in his call as being due to general skepticism on the part of the plant official, returned to his shack with a camera. They couldn't very well argue with a photograph, and he'd be hornswoggled if he'd show them the real thing before they came across with the cash.

AL-76 was busy with affairs of his own. Half of the contents of Payne's shack was littered over about two acres of ground, and in the middle of it the robot squatted and fooled around with radio tubes, hunks of iron, copper wire, and general junk. He paid no attention to Payne, who, sprawling flat on his belly, focused his camera for a beautiful shot.

And at this point it was that Lemuel Oliver Cooper turned the bend in the road and froze in his tracks as he took in the tableau. The reason for his coming in the first place was an ailing electric toaster that had developed the annoying habit of throwing out pieces of bread forcefully, but thoroughly untoasted. The reason for his *leaving* was more obvious. He had come with a slow, mildly cheerful, spring-morning saunter. He left with a speed that would have caused any college track coach to raise his eyebrows and purse his lips approvingly.

There was no appreciable slackening of speed until Cooper hurtled into Sheriff Saunders' office, minus hat and toaster, and brought himself up hard against the wall.

Kindly hands lifted him, and for half a minute he tried speaking before he had actually calmed down to the point of breathing with, of course, no result.

They gave him whisky and fanned him and when he did speak, it came out something like this: "—monster—seven feet tall—shack all busted up—poor Rannie Payne—" and so on.

They got the story out of him gradually: how there was a huge metal monster, seven feet tall, maybe even eight or nine, out at Randolph Payne's shack; how Randolph Payne himself was on his stomach, a "poor, bleeding, mangled corpse"; how the monster was then busily engaged in wrecking the shack out of sheer destructiveness; how it had turned on Lemuel Oliver Cooper, and how he, Cooper, had made his escape by half a hair.

Sheriff Saunders hitched his belt tighter about his portly middle and said, "It's that there machine man that got away from the Petersboro factory. We got warning on it last Saturday. Hey, Jake, you get every man in Hannaford County that can shoot and slap a deputy's badge on him. Get them here at noon. And listen, Jake, before you do that, just drop in at the Widow Payne's place and lip her the bad news gentle-like."

It is reported that Miranda Payne, upon being acquainted with events, paused only to make sure that her husband's insurance policy was safe, and to make a few pithy remarks concerning her foolishness in not having had him take out double the amount, before breaking out into as prolonged and heart-wringing a wail of grief as ever became a respectable widow.

It was some hours later that Randolph Payne—unaware of his horrible mutilation and death—viewed the completed negatives of his snapshots with satisfaction. As a series of portraits of a robot at work, they left nothing to the imagination. They might have been labeled: "Robot Gazing Thoughtfully at Vacuum Tube," "Robot Splicing Two Wires," "Robot Wielding Screwdriver," "Robot Taking Refrigerator Apart with Great Violence," and so on.

As there now remained only the routine of making the prints themselves, he stepped out from beyond the curtain of the improvised darkroom for a bit of a smoke and a chat with AL-76.

In doing so, he was blissfully unaware that the neighboring woods were verminous with nervous farmers armed with anything from an old colonial relic of a blunderbuss to the portable machine gun carried by the sheriff himself. Nor, for that matter, had he any inkling of the fact that half a dozen roboticists, under the leadership of Sam Tobe, were smoking down the highway from Petersboro at better than a hundred and twenty miles an hour for the sole purpose of having the pleasure and honor of his acquaintance.

So while things were jittering toward a climax, Randolph Payne sighed with self-satisfaction, lighted a match upon the seat of his pants, puffed away at his pipe, and looked at AL-76 with amusement.

It had been apparent for quite some time that the robot was more than slightly lunatic. Randolph Payne was himself an expert at homemade contraptions, having built several that could not have been exposed to daylight without searing the eyeballs of all beholders; but he had never even conceived of anything approaching the monstrosity that AL-76 was concocting.

It would have made the Rube Goldbergs of the day die in convulsions of envy. It would have made Picasso (if he could have lived to witness it) quit art in the sheer knowledge that he had been hopelessly surpassed. It would have soured the milk in the udders of any cow within half a mile.

In fact, it was gruesome!

From a rusty and massive iron base that faintly resembled something Payne had once seen attached to a secondhand tractor, it rose upward in rakish, drunken swerves through a bewildering mess of wires, wheels, tubes, and nameless horrors without number, ending in a megaphone arrangement that looked decidedly sinister.

Payne had the impulse to peek in the megaphone part, but refrained. He had seen far more sensible machines explode suddenly and with violence.

He said, "Hey, Al."

The robot looked up. He had been lying flat on his stomach, teasing a thin sliver of metal into place. "What do you want, Payne?"

"What is this?" He asked it in the tone of one referring to something foul and decomposing, held gingerly between two ten-foot poles.

"It's the Disinto I'm making—so I can start to work. It's an improvement on the standard model." The robot rose, dusted his knees clankingly, and looked at it proudly.

Payne shuddered. An "improvement"! No wonder they hid the original in caverns on the moon. Poor satellite! Poor dead satellite! He had always wanted to know what a fate worse than death was. Now he knew.

"Will it work?" he asked.

"Sure."

"How do you know?"

"It's got to. I made it, didn't I? I only need one thing now. Got a flashlight?"

"Somewhere, I guess." Payne vanished into the shack and returned almost immediately.

The robot unscrewed the bottom and set to work. In five minutes he had finished. He stepped back and said, "All set. Now I get to work. You may watch if you want to."

A pause, while Payne tried to appreciate the magnanimity of the offer. "Is it safe?"

"A baby could handle it."

"Oh!" Payne grinned weakly and got behind the thickest tree in the vicinity. "Go ahead," he said, "I have the utmost confidence in you."

AL-76 pointed to the nightmarish junk pile and said, "Watch!" His hands set to work—

The embattled farmers of Hannaford County, Virginia, weaved up upon Payne's shack in a slowly tightening circle. With the blood of their heroic colonial forebears pounding their veins—and goose flesh trickling up and down their spines—they crept from tree to tree.

Sheriff Saunders spread the word. "Fire when I give the signal—and aim at the eyes."

Jacob Linker—Lank Jake to his friends, and Sheriff's Deputy to himself—edged close. "You think maybe this machine man has skedaddled?" He did not quite manage to suppress the tone of wistful hopefulness in his voice.

"Dunno," grunted the sheriff. "Guess not, though. We woulda come across him in the woods if he had, and we haven't."

"But it's awful quiet, and it appears to me as if we're getting close to Payne's place."

The reminder wasn't necessary. Sheriff Saunders had a lump in his throat so big it had to be swallowed in three installments. "Get back," he ordered, "and keep your finger on the trigger."

They were at the rim of the clearing now, and Sheriff Saunders closed his eyes and stuck the corner of one out from behind the tree. Seeing nothing, he paused, then tried again, eyes open this time.

Results were, naturally, better.

To be exact, he saw one huge machine man, back toward him, bending over one soul-curdling, hiccupy contraption of uncertain origin and less certain purpose. The only item he missed was the quivering figure of Randolph Payne, embracing the tree next but three to the nor'-nor'west.

Sheriff Saunders stepped out into the open and raised his machine gun. The robot, still presenting a broad metal back, said in a loud voice—to person or persons unknown—"Watch!" and as the sheriff opened his mouth to signal a general order to fire, metal fingers compressed a switch.

There exists no adequate description of what occurred afterward, in spite of the presence of seventy eyewitnesses. In the days, months, and years to come not one of those seventy ever had a word to say about the few seconds after the sheriff had opened his mouth to give the firing order. When questioned about it, they merely turned apple-green and staggered away.

It is plain from circumstantial evidence, however, that, in a general way, what did occur was this.

Sheriff Saunders opened his mouth; AL-76 pulled a switch. The Disinto worked, and seventy-five trees, two barns, three cows and the top three quarters of Duckbill Mountain whiffed into rarefied atmosphere. They became, so to speak, one with the snows of yesteryear.

Sheriff Saunders' mouth remained open for an indefinite interval thereafter, but nothing—neither firing orders nor anything else—issued therefrom. And then—

And then, there was a stirring in the air, a multiple ro-o-o-oshing sound, a series of purple streaks through the atmosphere radiating away from Randolph Payne's shack as the center, and of the members of the posse, not a sign.

There were various guns scatttered about the vicinity, including the sheriff's patented nickel-plated, extra-rapid-fire, guaranteed-no-clog, portable machine gun. There were about fifty hats, a few half-chomped cigars, and some odds and ends that had come loose in the excitement—but of actual human beings there was none.

Except for Lank Jake, not one of those human beings came within human ken for three days, and the exception in his favor came about because he was interrupted in his comet-flight by the half-dozen men from the Petersboro factory, who were charging *into* the wood at a pretty fair speed of their own.

It was Sam Tobe who stopped him, catching Lank Jake's head skillfully in the pit of his stomach. When he caught his breath, Tobe asked, "Where's Randolph Payne's place?"

Lank Jake allowed his eyes to unglaze for just a moment. "Brother," he said, "just you follow the direction I ain't going."

And with that, miraculously, he was gone. There was a shrinking dot dodging trees on the horizon that might have been he, but Sam Tobe wouldn't have sworn to it.

That takes care of the posse; but there still remains Randolph Payne, whose reactions took something of a different form.

For Randolph Payne, the five-second interval after the pulling of the switch and the disappearance of Duckbill Mountain was a total blank. At the start he had been peering through the thick underbrush from behind the bottom of the trees; at the end he was swinging wildly from one of the topmost branches. The same impulse that had driven the posse horizontally had driven him vertically.

As to how he had covered the fifty feet from roots to top—whether he had climbed, jumped, or flown—he did not know, and he didn't give a particle of never-mind.

What he *did* know was that property had been destroyed by

a robot temporarily in his possession. All visions of rewards vanished and were replaced by trembling nightmares of hostile citizenry, shrieking lynch mobs, lawsuits, murder charges, and what Mirandy Payne would say. Mostly what Mirandy Payne would say.

He was yelling wildly and hoarsely, "Hey, you robot, you smash that thing, do you hear? Smash it good! You forget I ever had anything to do with it. You're a stranger to me, see? You don't ever say a word about it. Forget it, you hear?"

He didn't expect his orders to do any good; it was only reflex action. What he didn't know was that a robot always obeys a human order except where carrying it out involves danger to another human.

AL-76, therefore, calmly and methodically proceeded to demolish his Disinto into rubble and flinders.

Just as he was stamping the last cubic inch under foot, Sam Tobe and his contingent arrived, and Randolph Payne, sensing that the real owners of the robot had come, dropped out of the tree head-first and made for regions unknown feet-first.

He did not wait for his reward.

Austin Wilde, Robotical Engineer, turned to Sam Tobe and said, "Did you get anything out of the robot?"

Tobe shook his head and snarled deep in his throat. "Nothing. Not one thing. He's forgotten everything that's happened since he left the factory. He must have gotten *orders* to forget, or it couldn't have left him so blank. What was that pile of junk he'd been fooling with?"

"Just that. A pile of junk! But it must have been a Disinto before he smashed it, and I'd like to kill the fellow who ordered him to smash it—by slow torture, if possible. Look at this!"

They were part of the way up the slopes of what had been Duckbill Mountain—at that point, to be exact, where the top had been sheered off; and Wilde put his hand down upon the perfect flatness that cut through both soil and rock.

"What a Disinto," he said. "It took the mountain right off its base."

"What made him build it?"

Wilde shrugged. "I don't know. Some factor in his environment—there's no way of knowing what—reacted upon his moon-type positronic brain to produce a Disinto out of junk.

It's a billion to one against our ever stumbling upon that factor again now that the robot himself has forgotten. We'll never have that Disinto."

"Never mind. The important thing is that we have the robot."

"The hell you say." There was poignant regret in Wilde's voice. "Have you ever had anything to do with the Disintos on the moon? They eat up energy like so many electronic hogs and won't even begin to run until you've built up a potential of better than a million volts. But *this* Disinto worked differently. I went through the rubbish with a microscope, and would you like to see the only source of power of any kind that I found?"

"What was it?"

"Just this! And we'll never know how he did it."

And Austin Wilde held up the source of power that had enabled a Disinto to chew up a mountain in half a second—*two flashlight batteries!*

Victory Unintentional

Introduction

The next example is less blatantly humorous but is one in which the robots are still not taken quite seriously. The story arose out of another story—not about robots—to which the robot story served as sequel.

In the October 1941 issue of Astounding Science Fiction *was published a story of mine called "Not Final," in which the human colonists on Ganymede (largest of the satellites of Jupiter) make radio contact with life forms on Jupiter. These life forms turn out to be madly hostile and Earthmen begin to fear for their safety if the Jovians ever achieve space travel.*

To be sure, Jupiter's gravity is so intense and its atmosphere is so dense that spaceships of ordinary matter could not hold that atmosphere against the vacuum of space or lift itself against the gravity. However, human technology has developed force fields, and if the Jovians did the same, then they might emerge from their planet behind walls of sheer energy, rather than walls of matter.

It was necessary to investigate this point, but no human

beings could possibly have survived a trip to Jupiter's fantastically unfriendly surface.

However, if human beings can't do it, robots built by human beings can. With this in mind I wrote "Victory Unintentional," which appeared first in the August 1942 issue of Super Sciences Stories.

Victory Unintentional

The spaceship leaked, as the saying goes, like a sieve.

It was supposed to. In fact, that was the whole idea.

The result, of course, was that during the journey from Ganymede to Jupiter, the ship was crammed just as full as it could be with the very hardest space vacuum. And since the ship also lacked heating devices, this space vacuum was at normal temperature, which is a fraction of a degree above absolute zero.

This, also, was according to plan. Little things like the absence of heat and air didn't annoy anyone at all on the particular spaceship.

The first near vacuum wisps of Jovian atmosphere began percolating into the ship several thousand miles above the Jovian surface. It was practically all hydrogen, though perhaps a careful gas analysis might have located a trace of helium as well. The pressure gauges began creeping skyward.

That creep continued at an accelerating pace as the ship

dropped downward in a Jupiter-circling spiral. The pointers of successive gauges, each designed for progressively higher pressures, began to move until they reached the neighborhood of a million or so atmospheres, where figures lost most of their meaning. The temperature, as recorded by thermo-couples, rose slowly and erratically, and finally steadied at about seventy below zero, Centigrade.

The ship moved slowly toward the end, plowing its way heavily through a maze of gas molecules that crowded together so closely that hydrogen itself was squeezed to the density of a liquid. Ammonia vapor, drawn from the incredibly vast oceans of that liquid, saturated the horrible atmosphere. The wind, which had begun a thousand miles higher, had risen to a pitch inadequately described as a hurricane.

It was quite plain long before the ship landed on a fairly large Jovian island, perhaps seven times the size of Asia, that Jupiter was not a very pleasant world.

And yet the three members of the crew thought it was. They were quite convinced it was. But then, the three members of the crew were not exactly human. And neither were they exactly Jovian.

They were simply robots, designed on Earth for Jupiter.

ZZ Three said, "It appears to be a rather desolate place."

ZZ Two joined him and regarded the wind-blasted landscape somberly. "There are structures of some sort in the distance," he said, "which are obviously artificial. I suggest we wait for the inhabitants to come to us."

Across the room ZZ One listened, but made no reply. He was the first constructed of the three, and half experimental. Consequently he spoke a little less frequently than his two companions.

The wait was not long. An air vessel of queer design swooped overhead. More followed. And then a line of ground vehicles approached, took position, and disgorged organisms. Along with these organisms came various inanimate accessories that might have been weapons. Some of these were borne by a single Jovian, some by several, and some advanced under their own power, with Jovians perhaps inside.

The robots couldn't tell.

ZZ Three said, "They're all around us now. The logical

, peaceful gesture would be to come out in the open. Agreed?"

It was, and ZZ One shoved open the heavy door, which was not double or, for that matter, particularly airtight.

Their appearance through the door was the signal for an excited stir among the surrounding Jovians. Things were done to several of the very largest of the inanimate accessories, and ZZ Three became aware of a temperature rise on the outer rind of his beryllium-iridium-bronze body.

He glanced at ZZ Two. "Do you feel it? They're aiming heat energy at us, I believe."

ZZ Two indicated his surprise. "I wonder why?"

"Definitely a heat ray of some sort. Look at that!"

One of the rays had been jarred out of alignment for some undiscernible cause, and its line of radiation intersected a brook of sparkling pure ammonia—which promptly boiled furiously.

Three turned to ZZ One, "Make a note of this, One, will you?"

"Sure." It was to ZZ One that the routine secretarial work fell, and his method of taking a note was to make a mental addition to the accurate memory scroll within him. He had already gathered the hour-by-hour record of every important instrument on board ship during the trip to Jupiter. He added agreeably, "What reason shall I put for the reaction? The human masters would probably enjoy knowing."

"No reason. Or better," Three corrected himself, "no apparent reason. You might say the maximum temperature of the ray was about plus thirty, Centigrade."

Two interrupted, "Shall we try communicating?"

"It would be a waste of time," said Three. "There can't be more than a very few Jovians who know the radio-click code that's been developed between Jupiter and Ganymede. They'll have to send for one, and when he comes, he'll establish contact soon enough. Meanwhile let's watch them. I don't understand their actions, I tell you frankly."

Nor did understanding come immediately. Heat radiation ceased, and other instruments were brought to the forefront and put into play. Several capsules fell at the feet of the watching robots, dropping rapidly and forcefully under Jupiter's gravity. They popped open and a blue liquid exuded, forming pools which proceeded to shrink rapidly by evaporation.

The nightmare wind whipped the vapors away and where those vapors went, Jovians scrambled out of the way. One was too slow, threshed about wildly, and became very limp and still.

ZZ Two bent, dabbed a finger in one of the pools and stared at the dripping liquid. "I think this is oxygen," he said.

"Oxygen, all right," agreed Three. "This becomes stranger and stranger. It must certainly be a dangerous practice, for I would say that oxygen is poisonous to the creatures. One of them died!"

There was a pause, and then ZZ One, whose greater simplicity led at times to an increased directness of thought, said heavily, "It might be that these strange creatures in a rather childish way are attempting to destroy us."

And Two, struck by the suggestion, answered, "You know, One, I think you're right!"

There had been a slight lull in Jovian activity and now a new structure was brought up. It possessed a slender rod that pointed skyward through the impenetrable Jovian murk. It stood in that starkly incredible wind with a rigidity that plainly indicated remarkable structural strength. From its tip came a cracking and then a flash that lit up the depths of the atmosphere into a gray fog.

For a moment the robots were bathed in clinging radiance and then Three said thoughtfully, "High-tension electricity! Quite respectable power, too. One, I think you're right. After all, the human masters have told us that these creatures seek to destroy all humanity, and organisms possessing such insane viciousness as to harbor a thought of harm against a human being"—his voice trembled at the thought—"would scarcely scruple at attempting to destroy us."

"It's a shame to have such distorted minds," said ZZ One. "Poor fellows!"

"I find it a very saddening thought," admitted Two. "Let's go back to the ship. We've seen enough for now."

They did so, and settled down to wait. As ZZ Three said, Jupiter was a roomy planet, and it might take time for Jovian transportation to bring a radio code expert to the ship. However, patience is a cheap commodity to robots.

As a matter of fact, Jupiter turned on its axis three times, according to chronometer, before the expert arrived. The rising and setting of the sun made no difference, of course, to the dead darkness at the bottom of three thousand miles of liquid-dense gas, so that one could not speak of day and night. But then, neither Jovian nor robot saw by visible light radiation and that didn't matter.

Through this thirty-hour interval the surrounding Jovians continued their attack with a patience and persevering relent-lessness concerning which robot ZZ One made a good many mental notes. The ship was assaulted by as many varieties of forces as there were hours, and the robots observed every attack attentively, analyzing such weapons as they recognized. They by no means recognized all.

But the human masters had built well. It had taken fifteen years to construct the ship and the robots, and their essentials could be expressed in a single phrase—raw strength. The attack spent itself uselessly and neither ship nor robot seemed the worse for it.

Three said, "This atmosphere handicaps them, I think. They can't use atomic disruptors, since they would only tear a hole in that soupy air and blow themselves up."

"They haven't used high explosives either," said Two, "which is well. They couldn't have hurt us, naturally, but it would have thrown us about a bit."

"High explosives are out of the question. You can't have an explosive without gas expansion and gas just can't expand in this atmosphere."

"It's a very good atmosphere," muttered One. "I like it."

Which was natural, because he was built for it. The ZZ robots were the first robots ever turned out by the United States Robots and Mechanical Men Corporation that were not even faintly human in appearance. They were low and squat, with a center of gravity less than a foot above ground level. They had six legs apiece, stumpy and thick, designed to lift tons against two and a half times normal Earth gravity. Their re-flexes were that many times Earth-normal speed, to make up for the gravity. And they were composed of a beryllium-irid-ium-bronze alloy that was proof against any known corrosive agent, also any known destructive agent short of a thousand-megaton atomic disruptor, under any conditions whatsoever.

To dispense with further description, they were indestructible, and so impressively powerful that they were the only robots ever built on whom the roboticists of the corporation had never quite had the nerve to pin a serial-number nickname. One bright young fellow had suggested Sissy One, Two, and Three—but not in a very loud voice, and the suggestion was never repeated.

The last hours of the wait were spent in a puzzled discussion to find a possible description of a Jovian's appearance. ZZ One had made a note of their possession of tentacles and of their radial symmetry—and there he had stuck. Two and Three did their best, but couldn't help.

"You can't very well describe anything," Three declared finally, "without a standard of reference. These creatures are like nothing I know of—completely outside the positronic paths of my brain. It's like trying to describe gamma light to a robot unequipped for gamma-ray reception."

It was just at that time that the weapon barrage ceased once more. The robots turned their attention to outside the ship.

A group of Jovians were advancing in curiously uneven fashion, but no amount of careful watching could determine the exact method of their locomotion. How they used their tentacles was uncertain. At times the organisms took on a remarkable slithering motion, and then they moved at great speed, perhaps with the wind's help, for they were moving downwind.

The robots stepped out to meet the Jovians, who halted ten feet away. Both sides remained silent and motionless.

ZZ Two said, "They must be watching us, but I don't know how. Do either of you see any photosensitive organs?"

"I can't say," grunted Three in response. "I don't see anything about them that makes sense at all."

There was a sudden metallic clicking from among the Jovian group and ZZ One said delightedly, "It's the radio code. They've got the communications expert here."

It was, and they had. The complicated dot-dash system that over a period of twenty-five years had been laboriously developed by the beings of Jupiter and the Earthmen of Ganymede into a remarkably flexible means of communication was finally being put into practice at close range.

One Jovian remained in the forefront now, the others having fallen back. It was he that was speaking. The clicking said, "Where are you from?"

ZZ Three, as the most mentally advanced, naturally assumed spokesmanship for the robot group. "We are from Jupiter's satellite, Ganymede."

The Jovian continued, "What do you want?"

"Information. We have come to study your world and to bring back our findings. If we could have your cooperation—"

The Jovian clicking interrupted. "You must be destroyed!"

ZZ Three paused and said in a thoughtful aside to his two companions, "Exactly the attitude the human masters said they would take. They are very unusual."

Returning to his clicking, he asked simply, "Why?"

The Jovian evidently considered certain questions too obnoxious to be answered. He said, "If you leave within a single period of revolution, we will spare you—until such time as we emerge from our world to destroy the un-Jovian vermin of Ganymede."

"I would like to point out," said Three, "that we of Ganymede and the inner planets—"

The Jovian interrupted, "Our astronomy knows of the Sun and of our four satellites. There are no inner planets."

Three conceded the point wearily, "We of Ganymede, then. We have no designs on Jupiter. We're prepared to offer friendship. For twenty-five years your people communicated freely with the human beings of Ganymede. Is there any reason to make sudden war upon the humans?"

"For twenty-five years," was the cold response, "we assumed the inhabitants of Ganymede to be Jovians. When we found out they were not, and that we had been treating lower animals on the scale of Jovian intelligences, we were bound to take steps to wipe out the dishonor."

Slowly and forcefully he finished, "We of Jupiter will suffer the existence of no vermin!"

The Jovian was backing away in some fashion, tacking against the wind, and the interview was evidently over.

The robots retreated inside the ship.

ZZ Two said, "It looks bad, doesn't it?" He continued thoughtfully, "It is as the human masters said. They possess an ultimately developed superiority complex, combined with an extreme intolerance for anyone or anything that disturbs that complex."

"The intolerance," observed Three, "is the natural consequence of the complex. The trouble is that their intolerance has teeth in it. They have weapons—and their science is great."

"I am not surprised now," burst out ZZ One, "that we were specifically instructed to disregard Jovian orders. They are horrible, intolerant, pseudo-superior beings!" He added emphatically, with robotical loyalty and faith, "No human master could ever be like that."

"That, though true, is beside the point," said Three. "The fact remains that the human masters are in terrible danger. This is a gigantic world and these Jovians are greater in numbers and resources by a hundred times or more than the humans of the entire Terrestrial Empire. If they can ever develop the force field to the point where they can use it as a spaceship hull— as the human masters have already done—they will overrun the system at will. The question remains as to how far they have advanced in that direction, what other weapons they have, what preparations they are making, and so on. To return with that information is our function, of course, and we had better decide on our next step."

"It may be difficult," said Two. "The Jovians won't help us." Which, at the moment, was rather an understatement.

Three thought awhile. "It seems to me that we need only wait," he observed. "They have tried to destroy us for thirty hours now and haven't succeeded. Certainly they have done their best. Now a superiority complex always involves the eternal necessity of saving face, and the ultimatum given us proves it in this case. They would never allow us to leave if they could destroy us. But if we don't leave, then rather than admit they cannot force us away, they will surely pretend that they are willing, for their own purposes, to have us stay."

Once again they waited. The day passed. The weapon barrage did not resume. The robots did not leave. The bluff was called. And now the robots faced the Jovian radio-code expert once again.

If the ZZ models had been equipped with a sense of humor, they would have enjoyed themselves immensely. As it was, they felt merely a solemn sense of satisfaction.

The Jovian said, "It has been our decision that you will be allowed to remain for a very short time, so that you see our power for yourself. You shall then return to Ganymede to inform your companion vermin of the disastrous end to which they will unfailingly come within a solar revolution."

ZZ One made a mental note that a Jovian revolution took twelve earthly years.

Three replied casually, "Thank you. May we accompany you to the nearest town? There are many things we would like to learn." He added as an afterthought, "Our ship is not to be touched, of course."

He said this as a request, not as a threat, for no ZZ model was ever pugnacious. All capacity for even the slightest annoyance had been carefully barred in their construction. With robots as vastly powerful as the ZZs, unfailing good temper was essential for safety during the years of testing on Earth.

The Jovian said, "We are not interested in your verminous ship. No Jovian will pollute himself by approaching it. You may accompany us, but you must on no account approach closer than ten feet to any Jovian, or you will be instantly destroyed."

"Stuck up, aren't they?" observed Two in a genial whisper, as they plowed into the wind.

The town was a port on the shores of an incredible ammonia lake. The external wind whipped furious, frothy waves that shot across the liquid surface at the hectic rate enforced by the gravity. The port itself was neither large nor impressive and it seemed fairly evident that most of the construction was underground.

"What is the population of this place?" asked Three.

The Jovian replied, "It is a small town of ten million."

"I see. Make a note of that, One."

ZZ One did so mechanically, and then turned once more to the lake, at which he had been staring in fascination. He pulled at Three's elbow. "Say, do you suppose they have fish here?"

"What difference does it make?"

"I think we ought to know. The human masters ordered us to find out everything we could." Of the robots, One was the simplest and, consequently, the one who took orders in the most literal fashion.

Two said, "Let One go and look if he likes. It won't do any harm if we let the kid have his fun."

"All right. There's no real objection if he doesn't waste his time. Fish aren't what we came for—but go ahead, One."

ZZ One made off in great excitement and slogged rapidly down the beach, plunging into the ammonia with a splash. The Jovians watched attentively. They had understood none of the previous conversation, of course.

The radio code expert clicked out, "It is apparent that your companion has decided to abandon life in despair at our greatness."

Three said in surprise, "Nothing of the sort. He wants to investigate the living organisms, if any, that live in the ammonia." He added apologetically, "Our friend is very curious at times, and he isn't quite as bright as we are, though that is only his misfortune. We understand that and try to humor him whenever we can."

There was a long pause, and the Jovian observed, "He will drown."

Three replied casually, "No danger of that. We don't drown. May we enter the town as soon as he returns?"

At that moment there was a spurt of liquid several hundred feet out in the lake. It sprayed upward wildly and then hurtled down in a wind-driven mist. Another spurt and another, then a wild white foaming that formed a trail toward shore, gradually quieting as it approached.

The two robots watched this in amazement, and the utter lack of motion on the part of the Jovians indicated that they were watching as well.

Then the head of ZZ One broke the surface and he made his slow way out on to dry land. But something followed him! Some organism of gigantic size that seemed nothing but fangs, claws, and spines. Then they saw that it wasn't following him under its own power, but was being dragged across the beach by ZZ One. There was a significant flabbiness about it.

ZZ One approached rather timidly and took communication into his own hands. He tapped out a message for the Jovian in agitated fashion. "I am very sorry this happened, but the thing attacked me. I was merely taking notes on it. It is not a valuable creature, I hope."

He was not answered immediately, for at the first appearance of the monster there had been a wild break in the Jovian ranks. These re-formed slowly, and cautious observation having proven

the creature to be indeed dead, order was restored. Some of
the bolder were curiously prodding the body.

ZZ Three said humbly, "I hope you will pardon our friend.
He is sometimes clumsy. We have absolutely no intention of
harming any Jovian creature."

"He attacked me," explained One. "He bit at me without
provocation. See!" And he displayed a two-foot fang that ended
in a jagged break. "He broke it on my shoulder and almost left
a scratch. I just slapped it a bit to send it away—and it died.
I'm sorry!"

The Jovian finally spoke, and his code clicking was a rather
stuttery affair. "It is a wild creature, rarely found so close to
shore, but the lake is deep just here."

Three said, still anxiously, "If you can use it for food, we
are only too glad—"

"No. We can get food for ourselves without the help of
verm—without the help of others. Eat it yourselves."

At that ZZ One heaved the creature up and back into the
sea, with an easy motion of one arm. Three said casually,
"Thank you for your kind offer, but we have no use for food.
We don't eat, of course."

Escorted by two hundred or so armed Jovians, the robots
passed down a series of ramps into the underground city. If,
above the surface, the city had looked small and unimpressive,
then from beneath it took on the appearance of a vast mega-
lopolis.

They were ushered into ground cars that were operated by
remote control—for no honest, self-respecting Jovian would
risk his superiority by placing himself in the same car with
vermin—and driven at frightful speed to the center of the town.
They saw enough to decide that it extended fifty miles from
end to end and reached downward into Jupiter's crust at least
eight miles.

ZZ Two did not sound happy as he said, "If this is a sample
of Jovian development then we shall not have a hopeful report
to bring back to the human masters. After all, we landed on
the vast surface of Jupiter at random, with the chances a thousand to one against coming near any really concentrated center
of population. This must be, as the code expert says, a mere
town."

"Ten million Jovians," said Three abstractedly. "Total pop-

ulation must be in the trillions, which is high, very high, even
for Jupiter. They probably have a completely urban civilization,
which means that their scientific development must be tre-
mendous. If they have force fields—"

Three had no neck, for in the interest of strength the heads
of the ZZ models were riveted firmly onto the torso, with the
delicate positronic brains protected by three separate layers in
inch-thick iridium alloy. But if he had had one, he would have
shaken his head dolefully.

They had stopped now in a cleared space. Everywhere about
them they could see avenues and structures crowded with Jovians, as curious as any terrestrial crowd would have been in
similar circumstances.

The code expert approached. "It is time now for me to retire
until the next period of activity. We have gone so far as to
arrange quarters for you at great inconvenience to ourselves
for, of course, the structure will have to be pulled down and
rebuilt afterward. Nevertheless, you will be allowed to sleep
for a space."

ZZ Three waved an arm in deprecation and tapped out, "We
thank you but you must not trouble yourself. We don't mind
remaining right here. If you want to sleep and rest, by all
means do. We'll wait for you. As for us," casually, "we don't
sleep."

The Jovian said nothing, though if it had had a face, the
expression upon it might have been interesting. It left, and the
robots remained in the car, with squads of well-armed Jovians,
frequently replaced, surrounding them as guards.

It was hours before the ranks of those guards parted to allow
the code expert to return. Along with him were other Jovians,
whom he introduced.

"There are with me two officials of the central government
who have graciously consented to speak with you."

One of the officials evidently knew the code, for his clicking
interrupted the code expert sharply. He addressed the robots,
"Vermin! Emerge from the ground car that we may look at
you."

The robots were only too willing to comply, so while Three
and Two vaulted over the right side of the car, ZZ One dashed
through the left side. The word through is used advisedly, for
since he neglected to work the mechanism that lowered a sec-

tion of side so that one might exit, he carried that side, plus two wheels and an axle, along with him. The car collapsed, and ZZ One stood staring at the ruins in embarrassed silence.

At last he clicked out gently, "I'm very sorry. I hope it wasn't an expensive car."

ZZ Two added apologetically, "Our companion is often clumsy. You must excuse him," and ZZ Three made a half-hearted attempt to put the car back together again.

ZZ One made another effort to excuse himself. "The material of the car was rather flimsy. You see?" He lifted a square-yard sheet of three-inch-thick, metal-hard plastic in both hands and exerted a bit of pressure. The sheet promptly snapped in two. "I should have made allowances," he admitted.

The Jovian government official said in slightly less sharp fashion, "The car would have had to be destroyed anyway, after being polluted by your presence." He paused, then, "Creatures! We Jovians lack vulgar curiosity concerning lower animals, but our scientists seek facts."

"We're right with you," replied Three cheerfully. "So do we."

The Jovian ignored him. "You lack the mass-sensitive organ, apparently. How is it that you are aware of distant objects?"

Three grew interested. "Do you mean your people are directly sensitive to mass?"

"I am not here to answer your questions—your impudent questions—about us."

"I take it then that objects of low specific mass would be transparent to you, even in the absence of radiation." He turned to Two, "That's how they see. Their atmosphere is as transparent as space to them."

The Jovian clicking began once more, "You will answer my first question immediately, or my patience will end and I will order you destroyed."

Three said at once, "We are energy-sensitive. We can adjust ourselves to the entire electromagnetic scale at will. At present, our long-distance sight is due to radio-wave radiation that we emit ourselves, and at close range we see by—" He paused, and said to Two, "There isn't any code word for gamma ray, is there?"

"Not that I know of," Two answered.

Three continued to the Jovian, "At close range we see by other radiation for which there is no code word."

"Of what is your body composed?" demanded the Jovian.

Two whispered, "He probably asks that because his mass sensitivity can't penetrate past our skin. High density, you know. Ought we to tell him?"

Three replied uncertainly, "Our human masters didn't particularly say we were to keep anything secret." In radio code, to the Jovian he said, "We are mostly iridium. For the rest, copper, tin, a little beryllium, and a scattering of other substances."

The Jovians fell back and by the obscure writhing of various portions of their thoroughly indescribable bodies gave the impression that they were in animated conversation, although they made no sound.

And then the official returned. "Beings of Ganymede! It has been decided to show you through some of our factories that we may exhibit a tiny part of our great achievements. We will then allow you to return so that you may spread despair among the other verm—the other beings of the outer world."

Three said to Two, "Note the effect of their psychology. They must hammer home their superiority. It's still a matter of saving face." And in radio code, "We thank you for the opportunity."

But the face saving was efficient, as the robots realized soon enough. The demonstration became a tour, and the tour a Grand Exhibition. The Jovians displayed everything, explained everything, answered all questions eagerly, and ZZ One made hundreds of despairing notes.

The war potential of that single so-called unimportant town was greater by several times than that of all Ganymede. Ten more such towns would outproduce all the Terrestrial Empire. Yet ten more such towns would not be the fingernail fragment of the strength all Jupiter must be able to exert.

Three turned as One nudged him. "What is it?"

ZZ One said seriously, "If they have force fields, the human masters are lost, aren't they?"

"I'm afraid so. Why do you ask?"

"Because the Jovians aren't showing us through the right wing of this factory. It might be that force fields are being developed there. They would be wanting to keep it secret if they were. We'd better find out. It's the main point, you know."

Three regarded One somberly. "Perhaps you're right. It's no use ignoring anything."

They were in a huge steel mill now, watching hundred-foot beams of ammonia-resistant silicon-steel alloy being turned out twenty to the second. Three asked quietly, "What does that wing contain?"

The government official inquired of those in charge of the factory and explained, "That is the section of great heat. Various processes require huge temperatures which life cannot bear, and they must all be handled indirectly."

He led the way to a partition from which heat could be felt to radiate and indicated a small, round area of transparent material. It was one of a row of such, through which the foggy red light of lines of glowing forges could be made out through the soupy atmosphere.

ZZ One fastened a look of suspicion on the Jovian and clicked out, "Would it be all right if I went in and looked around? I am very interested in this."

Three said, "You're being childish, One. They're telling the truth. Oh well, nose around if you must. But don't take too long; we've got to move on."

The Jovian said, "You have no understanding of the heat involved. You will die."

"Oh, no," explained One casually. "Heat doesn't bother us."

There was a Jovian conference, and then a scene of scurrying confusion as the life of the factory was geared to this unusual emergency. Screens of heat-absorbent material were set up, and then a door dropped open, a door that had never before budged while the forges were working. ZZ One entered and the door closed behind him. Jovian officials crowded to the transparent areas to watch.

ZZ One walked to the nearest forge and tapped the outside. Since he was too short to see into it comfortably, he tipped the forge until the molten metal licked at the lip of the container. He peered at it curiously, then dipped his hand in and stirred it awhile to test the consistency. Having done this, he withdrew his hand, shook off some of the fiery metallic droplets and wiped the rest on one of his six thighs. Slowly he went down the line of forges, then signified his desire to leave.

The Jovians retired to a great distance when he came out of the door and played a stream of ammonia on him, which hissed, bubbled and steamed until he was brought to bearable temperature once more.

ZZ One ignored the ammonia shower and said, "They were telling the truth. No force fields."

Three began, "You see—" but One interrupted impatiently, "But there's no use delaying. The human masters instructed us to find out everything and that's that."

He turned to the Jovian and clicked out, without the slightest hesitation, "Listen, has Jovian science developed force fields?"

Bluntness was, of course, one of the natural consequences of One's less well developed mental powers. Two and Three knew that, so they refrained from expressing disapproval of the remark.

The Jovian official relaxed slowly from his strangely stiffened attitude, which had somehow given the impression that he had been staring stupidly at One's hand—the one he had dipped into the molten metal. The Jovian said slowly, "Force fields? That, then, is your main object of curiosity?"

"Yes," said One with emphasis.

There was a sudden and patent gain in confidence on the Jovian's part, for the clicking grew sharper. "Then come, vermin!"

Whereupon Three said to Two, "We're vermin again, I see—which sounds as if there's bad news ahead." And Two gloomily agreed.

It was to the very edge of the city that they were now led— to the portion which on Earth would have been termed the suburbs—and into one of a series of closely integrated structures, which might have corresponded vaguely to a terrestrial university.

There were no explanations, however, and none was asked for. The Jovian official led the way rapidly, and the robots followed with the grim conviction that the worst was just about to happen.

It was ZZ One who stopped before an opened wall section after the rest had passed on. "What's this?" he wanted to know.

The room was equipped with narrow, low benches, along which Jovians manipulated rows of strange devices, of which strong, inch-long electromagnets formed the principal feature.

"What's this?" asked One again.

The Jovian turned back and exhibited impatience. "This is a students' biological laboratory. There's nothing there to interest you."

"But what are they doing?"

"They are studying microscopic life. Haven't you ever seen a microscope before?"

Three interrupted in explanation, "He has, but not that type. Our microscopes are meant for energy-sensitive organs and work by refraction of radiant energy. Your microscopes evidently work on a mass-expansion basis. Rather ingenious."

ZZ One said, "Would it be all right if I inspected some of your specimens?"

"Of what use will that be? You cannot use our microscopes because of your sensory limitations and it will simply force us to discard such specimens as you approach for no decent reason."

"But I don't need a microscope," explained One, with surprise. "I can easily adjust myself for microscopic vision."

He strode to the nearest bench, while the students in the room crowded to the corner in an attempt to avoid contamination. ZZ One shoved a microscope aside and inspected the slide carefully. He backed away, puzzled, then tried another . . . a third . . . a fourth.

He came back and addressed the Jovian. "Those are supposed to be alive, aren't they? I mean those little worm things."

The Jovian said, "Certainly."

"That's strange—when I look at them, they die!"

Three exclaimed sharply and said to his two companions, "We've forgotten our gamma-ray radiation. Let's get out of here, One, or we'll kill every bit of microscopic life in the room."

He turned to the Jovian, "I'm afraid that our presence is fatal to weaker forms of life. We had better leave. We hope the specimens are not too difficult to replace. And, while we're about it, you had better not stay too near us, or our radiation may affect you adversely. You feel all right so far, don't you?" he asked.

The Jovian led the way onward in proud silence, but it was to be noticed that thereafter he doubled the distance he had hitherto kept between himself and them.

Nothing more was said until the robots found themselves in

a vast room. In the very center of it huge ingots of metal rested unsupported in mid-air—or, rather, supported by nothing visible—against mighty Jovian gravity.

The Jovian clicked, "There is your force field in ultimate form, as recently perfected. Within that bubble is a vacuum, so that it is supporting the full weight of our atmosphere plus an amount of metal equivalent to two large spaceships. What do you say to that?"

"That space travel now becomes a possibility for you," said Three.

"Definitely. No metal or plastic has the strength to hold our atmosphere against a vacuum, but a force field can—and a force-field bubble will be our spaceship. Within the year we will be turning them out by the hundreds of thousands. Then we will swarm down upon Ganymede to destroy the verminous so-called intelligences that attempt to dispute our dominion of the universe."

"The human beings of Ganymede have never attempted—" began Three, in mild expostulation.

"Silence!" snapped the Jovian. "Return now and tell them what you've seen. Their own feeble force fields—such as the one your ship is equipped with—will not stand against us, for our smallest ship will be a hundred times the size and power of yours."

Three said, "Then there's nothing more to do and we will return, as you say, with the information. If you could lead us back to our ship, we'll say good-by. But by the way, just as a matter for the record, there's something you don't understand. The humans of Ganymede have force fields, of course, but our particular ship isn't equipped with one. We don't need any."

The robot turned away and motioned his companions to follow. For a moment they did not speak, then ZZ One muttered dejectedly, "Can't we try to destroy this place?"

"It won't help," said Three. "They'd get us by weight of numbers. It's no use. In an earthly decade the human masters will be finished. It is impossible to stand against Jupiter. There's just too much of it. As long as Jovians were tied to the surface, the humans were safe. But now that they have force fields— All we can do is to bring the news. By the preparation of hiding places, some few may survive for a short while."

The city was behind them. They were out on the open plain

by the lake, with their ship a dark spot on the horizon, when the Jovian spoke suddenly:

"Creatures, you say you have no force field?"

Three replied without interest, "We don't need one."

"How then does your ship stand the vacuum of space without exploding because of the atmospheric pressure within?" And he moved a tentacle as if in mute gesture at the Jovian atmosphere that was weighing down upon them with a force of twenty million pounds to the square inch.

"Well," explained Three, "that's simple. Our ship isn't airtight. Pressures equalize within and without."

"Even in space? A vacuum in your ship? You lie!"

"You're welcome to inspect our ship. It has no force field and it isn't airtight. What's marvelous about that? We don't breathe. Our energy is obtained through direct atomic power. The presence or absence of air pressure makes little difference to us and we're quite at home in a vacuum."

"But absolute zero!"

"It doesn't matter. We regulate our own heat. We're not interested in outside temperatures." He paused. "Well, we can make our own way back to the ship. Good-by. We'll give the humans of Ganymede your message—war to the end!"

But the Jovian said, "Wait! I'll be back." He turned and went toward the city.

The robots stared, and then waited in silence.

It was three hours before he returned and when he did, it was in breathless haste. He stopped within the usual ten feet of the robots, but then began inching his way forward in a curious groveling fashion. He did not speak until his rubbery gray skin was almost touching them, and then the radio code sounded, subdued and respectful.

"Honored sirs, I have been in communication with the head of our central government, who is now aware of all the facts, and I can assure you that Jupiter desires only peace."

"I beg your pardon?" asked Three blankly.

The Jovian drove on hastily. "We are ready to resume communication with Ganymede and will gladly promise to make no attempt to venture into space. Our force field will be used only on the Jovian surface."

"But—" Three began.

"Our government will be glad to receive any other representatives our honorable human brothers of Ganymede would care to send. If your honors will now condescend to swear peace—" a scaly tentacle swung out toward them and Three, quite dazed, grasped it. Two and One did likewise as two more were extended to them.

The Jovian said solemnly: "There is then eternal peace between Jupiter and Ganymede."

The spaceship which leaked like a sieve was out in space again. The pressure and temperature were once more at zero, and the robots watched the huge but steadily shrinking globe that was Jupiter.

"They're definitely sincere," said ZZ Two, "and it's very gratifying, this complete about-face, but I don't get it."

"It is my idea," observed ZZ One, "that the Jovians came to their senses just in time and realized the incredible evil involved in the thought of harm to a human master. That would be only natural."

ZZ Three sighed and said, "Look, it's all a matter of psychology. Those Jovians had a superiority complex a mile thick and when they couldn't destroy us, they were bound to save face. All their exhibitions, all their explanations, were simply a form of braggadocio, designed to impress us into the proper state of humiliation before their power and superiority."

"I see all that," interrupted Two, "but—"

Three went on, "But it worked the wrong way. All they did was to prove to themselves that we were stronger, that we didn't drown, that we didn't eat or sleep, that molten metal didn't hurt us. Even our very presence was fatal to Jovian life. Their last trump was the force field. And when they found out that *we* didn't need them at all, and could live in a vacuum at absolute zero, they broke." He paused and added philosophically, "When a superiority complex like that breaks, it breaks all the way."

The other two considered that, and then Two said, "But it still doesn't make sense. Why should they care what we can or can't do? We're only robots. We're not the ones they have to fight."

"And that's the whole point, Two," said Three softly. "It's only after we left Jupiter that I thought of it. Do you know that through an oversight, quite unintentionally, we neglected to tell them we were only robots."

"They never asked us," said One.

"Exactly. So they thought we were human beings and that all the other human beings were like us!"

He looked once more at Jupiter, thoughtfully. "No wonder they decided to quit!"

PART II

The Laws
of Robotics

First Law

Introduction

Neither Robot AL-76 nor Robot ZZ-3 represented the mainstream of my thinking. As a matter of fact, I had started correctly with my very earliest robot story, "Robbie," which appeared in the September 1940 *Super Science Stories* (under the editorially chosen, and to me personally distasteful, title of "Strange Playfellow").

"Robbie" dealt with a rather primitive model, one that was unable to speak. It was designed to fulfill the task of nursemaid and to fulfill it admirably. Far from being a threat to human beings or wanting to destroy its creator or to take over the world, it strove only to do what it was designed to do. (Does an automobile want to fly? Does an electric light bulb want to type letters?)

I trod this path in eight other stories written during the 1940s, all of which appeared in *Astounding Science Fiction*. They were:

> "Reason," April 1941
> "Liar!" May 1941

"Runaround," March 1942
"Catch That Rabbit," February 1944
"Paradoxical Escape," August 1945
"Evidence," September 1946
"Little Lost Robot," March 1947
"The Evitable Conflict," June 1950

These eight stories plus *"Robbie"* were brought to-gether in a collection entitled I, Robot, *which was pub-lished by Gnome Press in 1950. After the usual reprint and foreign editions, it was allowed to go out of print, whereupon the enterprising gentlemen of Doubleday & Company, recognizing a Good Thing, arranged to bring out a new edition in 1963.**

My sensible, non-Mephistophelean robots were not really brand-new. There had been occasional robots of this type before 1940. Indeed, we can find some robots, designed to fulfill a reasonable purpose without trouble and without danger, in the Iliad. In Book XVIII of that epic, Thetis visits the smith-god, Hephaistos, in order to obtain divinely forged armor for her son, Achilles. Hephaistos is lame and walks with difficulty. There is the passage (in the translation of W. H. D. Rouse) which describes how he comes out to meet Thetis:

"Then he...limped out leaning on a thick stick, with a couple of maids to support him. These are made of gold exactly like living girls; they have sense in their heads, they can speak and use their muscles, they can spin and weave and do their work..."

In short, they were robots.

And yet, though I wasn't the first in the field by the not-so-narrow margin of 2500 years, I managed to build enough consistent background into my stories to gain for myself the reputation of having created the "modern robot story."

Gradually, story by story, I evolved my notions on the

---

*Because of the recent appearance of this collection, it is not being included in this otherwise definitive collection of my robot stories. The discerning reader will now understand why this book is entitled EIGHT STORIES FROM THE REST OF THE ROBOTS.

subject. My robots had brains of platinum-iridium sponge and the "brain paths" were marked out by the production and destruction of positrons. (No, I don't know how this is done.) As a result it is as the "positronic robots" that my creatures came to be known.

To design the positronic brains of my robots required a huge and intricate new branch of technology to which I gave the name "robotics." To me it seemed a natural word, as natural as "physics" or "mechanics." However, rather to my surprise, it turned out to be an invented word and is not to be found in either the second or third edition of Webster's Unabridged.

Most important of all, I made use of what I called "The Three Laws of Robotics," which were intended to place in words the basic design of the robot brains, a basic design to which all else was subsidiary.

These laws are:

1-A robot may not injure a human being, or, through inaction, allow a human being to come to harm.

2-A robot must obey the orders given it by human beings except where such orders would conflict with the First Law.

3-A robot must protect its own existence as long as such protection does not conflict with the First or Second Law.

Apparently it is these laws of robotics (first stated explicitly in "Runaround") that have done most to change the nature of the robot stories in modern science fiction. It is rare that a robot of the old turning-on-its-creator type will be found between the pages of the better science-fiction magazines, simply because that would violate the First Law. Many writers of robot stories, without actually quoting the three laws, take them for granted and expect the readers to do the same.

In fact I have been told that if, in future years, I am to be remembered at all, it will be for these three laws of robotics. In a way this bothers me, for I am accustomed to thinking of myself as a scientist, and to be remembered for the non-existent basis of a non-existent science is embarrassing. Yet if robotics ever does reach the pitch of excellence described in my stories, it may be that something like the Three Laws will really come into existence and, if so, I will have achieved a rather unusual (if, alas, posthumous) triumph.

My positronic robot stories fall into two groups; those that concern Dr. Susan Calvin and those that do not. Those that do not, often deal with Gregory Powell and Mike Donovan, who were constantly field-testing experimental robots and, just as constantly, running into trouble with them. There was just enough ambiguity in the Three Laws to provide the conflicts and uncertainties required for new stories, and, to my great relief, it seemed always to be possible to think up a new angle out of the sixty-one words of the Three Laws.

Four stories in I, Robot dealt with Powell and Donovan. After that book was published, exactly one other such story was published, or rather a story about Donovan alone. Once again I was being funny at the expense of my robots, but this time it wasn't I that was telling the story, it was Donovan, and I am not responsible for him.

The story "First Law" appeared in the October 1956 issue of Fantastic Universe Science Fiction.

First Law

Mike Donovan looked at his empty beer mug, felt bored, and decided he had listened long enough. He said, loudly, "If we're going to talk about unusual robots, *I* once knew one that disobeyed the First Law."

And since that was completely impossible, everyone stopped talking and turned to look at Donovan.

Donovan regretted his big mouth at once and changed the subject. "I heard a good one yesterday," he said, conversationally, "about—"

MacFarlane in the chair next to Donovan's said, "You mean you knew a robot that harmed a human being?" That was what disobedience to First Law meant, of course.

"In a way," said Donovan. "I say I heard one about—"

"Tell us about it," ordered MacFarlane. Some of the others banged their beer mugs on the table.

Donovan made the best of it. "It happened on Titan about ten years ago," he said, thinking rapidly. "Yes, it was in twenty-five. We had just recently received a shipment of three new-model robots, specially designed for Titan. They were the first

53

of the MA models. We called them Emma One, Two and
Three." He snapped his fingers for another beer and stared
earnestly after the waiter. "Let's see, what came next?"

MacFarlane said, "I've been in robotics half my life, Mike.
I never heard of an MA serial order."

"That's because they took the MAs off the assembly lines
immediately after—after what I'm going to tell you. Don't
you remember?"

"No."

Donovan continued hastily. "We put the robots to work at
once. You see, until then, the Base had been entirely useless
during the stormy season, which lasts eighty percent of Titan's
revolution about Saturn. During the terrific snows, you couldn't
find the Base if it were only a hundred yards away. Compasses
aren't any use, because Titan hasn't any magnetic field.

"The virtue of these MA robots, however, was that they
were equipped with vibro-detectors of a new design so that
they could make a beeline for the Base through anything, and
that meant mining could become a through-the-revolution affair. And don't say a word, Mac. The vibro-detectors were
taken off the market also, and that's why you haven't heard
of them." Donovan coughed. "Military secret, you understand."

He went on. "The robots worked fine during the first stormy
season, then at the start of the calm season, Emma Two began
acting up. She kept wandering off into corners and under bales
and had to be coaxed out. Finally she wandered off Base altogether and didn't come back. We decided there had been a
flaw in her manufacture and got along with the other two. Still,
it meant we were short-handed, or short-roboted anyway, so
when toward the end of the calm season, someone had to go
to Kornsk, I volunteered to chance it without a robot. It seemed
safe enough; the storms weren't due for two days and I'd be
back in twenty hours at the outside.

"I was on the way back—a good ten miles from Base—
when the wind started blowing and the air thickening. I landed
my air car immediately before the wind could smash it, pointed
myself toward the Base and started running. I could run the
distance in the low gravity all right, but could I run a straight
line? That was the question. My air supply was ample and my
suit heat coils were satisfactory, but ten miles in a Titanian
storm is infinity.

"Then, when the snow streams changed everything to a dark, gooey twilight, with even Saturn dimmed out and the sun only a pale pimple, I stopped short and leaned against the wind. There was a little dark object right ahead of me. I could barely make it out but I knew what it was. It was a storm pup; the only living thing that could stand a Titanian storm, and the most vicious living thing anywhere. I knew my space suit wouldn't protect me, once it made for me, and in the bad light, I had to wait for a point-blank aim or I didn't dare shoot. One miss and he would be at me.

"I backed away slowly and the shadow followed. It closed in and I was raising my blaster, with a prayer, when a bigger shadow loomed over me suddenly, and I yodeled with relief. It was Emma Two, the missing MA robot. I never stopped to wonder what had happened to it or worry why it had. I just howled, 'Emma, baby, get that storm pup; and then get me back to Base.'

"It just looked at me as if it hadn't heard and called out, 'Master, don't shoot. Don't shoot.'

"It made for that storm pup at a dead run.

"'Get that damned pup, Emma,' I shouted. It got the pup, all right. It scooped it right up and *kept on going*. I yelled myself hoarse but it never came back. It left me to die in the storm."

Donovan paused dramatically, "Of course, you know the First Law: A robot may not injure a human being, or through in-action, allow a human being to come to harm! Well, Emma Two just ran off with that storm pup and left me to die. It broke First Law.

"Luckily, I pulled through safely. Half an hour later, the storm died down. It had been a premature gust, and a temporary one. That happens sometimes. I hot-footed it for Base and the storms really broke next day. Emma Two returned two hours after I did, and, of course, the mystery was then explained and the MA models were taken off the market immediately."

"And just what," demanded MacFarlane, "was the explanation?"

Donovan regarded him seriously. "It's true I was a human being in danger of death, Mac, but to that robot there was something else that came first, even before me, before the First Law. Don't forget these robots were of the MA series and this particular MA robot had been searching out private nooks for some time before disappearing. It was as though it expected something special—and private—to happen to it. Apparently, something special had."

Donovan's eyes turned upward reverently and his voice trembled. "That storm pup was no storm pup. We named it Emma Junior when Emma Two brought it back. Emma Two *had* to protect it from my gun. What is even First Law compared with the holy ties of mother love?"

Let's Get Together

*Another short story of the post-*I, Robot *decade was un-usual in that it was the first since the very early days that involved neither Susan Calvin nor the Powell-Donovan team. It was "Let's Get Together," which appeared in the February 1957 issue of* Infinity Science Fiction.

It was unusual in another way too. A couple of years after its appearance I received a reprint request, and (since I am easygoing to a fault) I said, "Sure!" When I finally received the issue of the magazine with the re-printed story, it turned out to be one of those magazines that feature the undraped female form divine.

Heaven knows I have no objection to divine forms, but the event left me with an unanswered question. Not only does "Let's Get Together" involve no sex, it has no female characters. Why did the magazine want it then?

Perhaps (I tell myself) because they thought it was a good story.

Maybe they did. At least, I hope so.

Let's Get Together

A kind of peace had endured for a century and people had forgotten what anything else was like. They would scarcely have known how to react had they discovered that a kind of war had finally come.

Certainly, Elias Lynn, Chief of the Bureau of Robotics, wasn't sure how he ought to react when *he* finally found out. The Bureau of Robotics was headquartered in Cheyenne, in line with the century-old trend toward decentralization, and Lynn stared dubiously at the young Security officer from Washington who had brought the news.

Elias Lynn was a large man, almost charmingly homely, with pale blue eyes that bulged a bit. Men weren't usually comfortable under the stare of those eyes, but the Security officer remained calm.

Lynn decided that his first reaction ought to be incredulity. Hell, it *was* incredulity! He just didn't believe it!

He eased himself back in his chair and said, "How certain is the information?"

The Security officer, who had introduced himself as Ralph

G. Breckenridge and had presented credentials to match, had the softness of youth about him; full lips, plump cheeks that flushed easily, and guileless eyes. His clothing was out of line with Cheyenne but it suited a universally air-conditioned Washington, where Security, despite everything, was still centered.

Breckenridge flushed and said, "There's no doubt about it."

"You people know all about Them, I suppose," said Lynn and was unable to keep a trace of sarcasm out of his tone. He was not particularly aware of his use of a slightly stressed pronoun in his reference to the enemy, the equivalent of capitalization in print. It was a cultural habit of this generation and the one preceding. No one said the "East," or the "Reds" or the "Soviets" or the "Russians" any more. That would have been too confusing, since some of Them weren't of the East, weren't Reds, Soviets, and especially not Russians. It was much simpler to say We and They, and much more precise.

Travelers had frequently reported that They did the same in reverse. Over there, They were "We" (in the appropriate language) and We were "They."

Scarcely anyone gave thought to such things any more. It was all quite comfortable and casual. There was no hatred, even. At the beginning, it had been called a Cold War. Now it was only a game, almost a good-natured game, with unspoken rules and a kind of decency about it.

Lynn said abruptly, "Why should They want to disturb the situation?"

He rose and stood staring at a wall map of the world, split into two regions with faint edgings of color. An irregular portion on the left of the map was edged in a mild green. A smaller, but just as irregular, portion on the right of the map was bordered in a washed-out pink. We and They.

The map hadn't changed much in a century. The loss of Formosa and the gain of East Germany some eighty years before had been the last territorial switch of importance.

There had been another change, though, that was significant enough and that was in the colors. Two generations before, Their territory had been a brooding, bloody red, Ours a pure and undefiled white. Now there was a neutrality about the colors. Lynn had seen Their maps and it was the same on Their side.

"They wouldn't do it," he said.

"They are doing it," said Breckenridge, "and you had better accustom yourself to the fact. Of course, sir, I realize that it isn't pleasant to think that They may be that far ahead of us in robotics."

His eyes remained as guileless as ever, but the hidden knife-edges of the words plunged deep, and Lynn quivered at the impact.

Of course, that would account for why the Chief of Robotics learned of this so late and through a Security officer at that. He had lost caste in the eyes of the Government; if Robotics had really failed in the struggle, Lynn could expect no political mercy.

Lynn said wearily, "Even if what you say is true, They're not far ahead of us. We could build humanoid robots."

"Have we, sir?"

"Yes. As a matter of fact, we have built a few models for experimental purposes."

"They were doing so ten years ago. They've made ten years' progress since."

Lynn was disturbed. He wondered if his incredulity concerning the whole business was really the result of wounded pride and fear for his job and reputation. He was embarrassed by the possibility that this might be so, and yet he was forced into defense.

He said, "Look, young man, the stalemate between Them and Us was never perfect in every detail, you know. They have always been ahead in one facet or another and We in some other facet or another. If They're ahead of us right now in robotics, it's because They've placed a greater proportion of Their effort into robotics than We have. And that means that some other branch of endeavor has received a greater share of Our efforts than it has of Theirs. It would mean We're ahead in force-field research or in hyperatomics, perhaps."

Lynn felt distressed at his own statement that the stalemate wasn't perfect. It was true enough, but that was the one great danger threatening the world. The world depended on the stalemate being as perfect as possible. If the small unevennesses that always existed overbalanced too far in one direction or the other—

Almost at the beginning of what had been the Cold War, both sides had developed thermonuclear weapons, and war became unthinkable. Competition switched from the military to the economic and psychological and had stayed there ever since.

But always there was the driving effort on each side to break the stalemate, to develop a parry for every possible thrust, to develop a thrust that could not be parried in time—something that would make war possible again. And that was not because either side wanted war so desperately, but because both were afraid that the other side would make the crucial discovery first.

For a hundred years each side had kept the struggle even. And in the process, peace had been maintained for a hundred years while, as byproducts of the continuously intensive research, force fields had been produced and solar energy and insect control and robots. Each side was making a beginning in the understanding of mentalics, which was the name given to the biochemistry and biophysics of thought. Each side had its outposts on the Moon and on Mars. Mankind was advancing in giant strides under forced draft.

It was even necessary for both sides to be as descent and humane as possible among themselves, lest through cruelty and tyranny, friends be made for the other side.

It couldn't be that the stalemate would now be broken and that there would be war.

Lynn said, "I want to consult one of my men. I want his opinion."

"Is he trustworthy?"

Lynn looked disgusted. "Good Lord, what man in Robotics has not been investigated and cleared to death by your people? Yes, I vouch for him. If you can't trust a man like Humphrey Carl Laszlo, then we're in no position to face the kind of attack you say They are launching, no matter what else we do."

"I've heard of Laszlo," said Breckenridge.

"Good. Does he pass?"

"Yes."

"Then, I'll have him in and we'll find out what he thinks about the possibility that robots could invade the U. S. A."

"Not exactly," said Breckenridge, softly. "You still don't accept the full truth. Find out what he thinks about the fact that robots have *already* invaded the U. S. A."

• • •

Laszlo was the grandson of a Hungarian who had broken through what had then been called the Iron Curtain, and he had a comfortable above-suspicion feeling about himself because of it. He was thick-set and balding with a pugnacious look graven forever on his snub face, but his accent was clear Harvard and he was almost excessively soft-spoken.

To Lynn, who was conscious that after years of administration he was no longer expert in the various phases of modern robotics, Laszlo was a comforting receptacle for complete knowledge. Lynn felt better because of the man's mere presence.

Lynn said, "What do you think?"

A scowl twisted Laszlo's face ferociously. "That They're that far ahead of us. Completely incredible. It would mean They've produced humanoids that could not be told from humans at close quarters. It would mean a considerable advance in robo-mentalics."

"You're personally involved," said Breckenridge, coldly. "Leaving professional pride out of account, exactly why is it impossible that They be ahead of Us?"

Laszlo shrugged. "I assure you that I'm well acquainted with Their literature on robotics. I know approximately where They are."

"You know approximately where They want you to *think* They are, is what you really mean," corrected Breckenridge. "Have you ever visited the other side?"

"I haven't," said Laszlo, shortly.

"Nor you, Dr. Lynn?"

Lynn said, "No, I haven't, either."

Breckenridge said, "Has any robotics man visited the other side in twenty-five years?" He asked the question with a kind of confidence that indicated he knew the answer.

For a matter of seconds, the atmosphere was heavy with thought. Discomfort crossed Laszlo's broad face. He said, "As a matter of fact, They haven't held any conferences on robotics in a long time."

"In twenty-five years," said Breckenridge. "Isn't that significant?"

"Maybe," said Laszlo, reluctantly. "Something else bothers me, though. None of Them have ever come to Our conferences on robotics. None that I can remember."

"Were They invited?" asked Breckenridge.

Lynn, staring and worried, interposed quickly, "Of course."

Breckenridge said, "Do They refuse attendance to any other types of scientific conferences We hold?"

"I don't know," said Laszlo. He was pacing the floor now. "I haven't heard of any cases. Have you, Chief?"

"No," said Lynn.

Breckenridge said, "Wouldn't you say it was as though They didn't want to be put in the position of having to return any such invitation? Or as though They were afraid one of Their men might talk too much?"

That was exactly how it seemed, and Lynn felt a helpless conviction that Security's story was true after all steal over him.

Why else had there been no contact between sides on robotics? There had been a cross-fertilizing trickle of researchers moving in both directions on a strictly one-for-one basis for years, dating back to the days of Eisenhower and Khrushchev. There were a great many good motives for that: an honest appreciation of the supranational character of science; impulses of friendliness that are hard to wipe out completely in the individual human being; the desire to be exposed to a fresh and interesting outlook and to have your own slightly stale notions greeted by others as fresh and interesting.

The governments themselves were anxious that this continue. There was always the obvious thought that by learning all you could and telling as little as you could, your own side would gain by the exchange.

But not in the case of robotics. Not there.

Such a little thing to carry conviction. And a thing, moreover, they had known all along. Lynn thought darkly: *We've taken the complacent way out.*

Because the other side had done nothing publicly on robotics, it had been tempting to sit back smugly and be comfortable in the assurance of superiority. Why hadn't it seemed possible, even likely, that They were hiding superior cards, a trump hand, for the proper time?

Laszlo said shakenly, "What do we do?" It was obvious that the same line of thought had carried the same conviction to him.

"Do?" parroted Lynn. It was hard to think right now of

anything but of the complete horror that came with conviction. There were ten humanoid robots somewhere in the United States, each one carrying a fragment of a TC bomb.

TC! The race for sheer horror in bomb-ery had ended there. TC! Total Conversion! The sun was no longer a synonym one could use. Total conversion made the sun a penny candle.

Ten humanoids, each completely harmless in separation, could, by the simple act of coming together, exceed critical mass and—

Lynn rose to his feet heavily, the dark pouches under his eyes, which ordinarily lent his ugly face a look of savage foreboding, more prominent than ever. "It's going to be up to us to figure out ways and means of telling a humanoid from a human and then finding the humanoids."

"How quickly?" muttered Laszlo.

"Not later than five minutes before they get together," barked Lynn, "and I don't know when that will be."

Breckenridge nodded. "I'm glad you're with us now, sir. I'm to bring you back to Washington for conference, you know."

Lynn raised his eyebrows. "All right."

He wondered if, had he delayed longer in being convinced, he might not have been replaced forthwith—if some other Chief of the Bureau of Robotics might not be conferring in Washington. He suddenly wished earnestly that exactly that had come to pass.

The First Presidential Assistant was there, the Secretary of Science, the Secretary of Security, Lynn himself, and Breckenridge. Five of them sitting about a table in the dungeons of an underground fortress near Washington.

Presidential Assistant Jeffreys was an impressive man, handsome in a white-haired and just-a-trifle-jowly fashion, solid, thoughtful and as unobtrusive, politically, as a Presidential Assistant ought to be.

He spoke incisively. "There are three questions that face us as I see it. First, when are the humanoids going to get together? Second, where are they going to get together? Third, how do we stop them before they get together?"

Secretary of Science Amberley nodded convulsively at that. He had been Dean of Northwestern Engineering before his appointment. He was thin, sharp-featured and noticeably edgy.

His forefingers traced slow circles on the table.

"As far as *when* they'll get together," he said. "I suppose it's definite that it won't be for some time."

"Why do you say that?" asked Lynn sharply.

"They've been in the U.S. at least a month already. So Security says."

Lynn turned automatically to look at Breckenridge, and Secretary of Security Macalaster intercepted the glance. Macalaster said, "The information is reliable. Don't get Breckenridge's apparent youth fool you, Dr. Lynn. That's part of his value to us. Actually, he's thirty-four and has been with the department for ten years. He has been in Moscow for nearly a year and without him, none of this terrible danger would be known to us. As it is, we have most of the details."

"Not the crucial ones," said Lynn.

Macalaster of Security smiled frostily. His heavy chin and close-set eyes were well-known to the public but almost nothing else about him was. He said, "We are all finitely human, Dr. Lynn. Agent Breckenridge has done a great deal."

Presidential Assistant Jeffreys cut in. "Let us say we have a certain amount of time. If action at the instant were necessary, it would have happened before this. It seems likely that they are waiting for a specific time. If we knew the place, perhaps the time would become self-evident.

"If they are going to TC a target, they will want to cripple us as much as possible, so it would seem that a major city would have to be it. In any case, a major metropolis is the only target worth a TC bomb. I think there are four possibilities: Washington, as the administrative center; New York, as the financial center; and Detroit and Pittsburgh as the two chief industrial centers."

Macalaster of Security said, "I vote for New York. Administration and industry have both been decentralized to the point where the destruction of any one particular city won't prevent instant retaliation."

"Then why New York?" asked Amberley of Science, perhaps more sharply than he intended. "Finance has been decentralized as well."

"A question of morale. It may be they intend to destroy our will to resist, to induce surrender by the sheer horror of the first blow. The greatest destruction of human life would be in the New York Metropolitan area—"

"Pretty cold-blooded," muttered Lynn.

"I know," said Macalaster of Security, "but they're capable of it, if they thought it would mean final victory at a stroke. Wouldn't we—"

Presidential Assistant Jeffreys brushed back his white hair. "Let's assume the worst. Let's assume that New York will be destroyed some time during the winter, preferably immediately after a serious blizzard when communications are at their worst and the disruption of utilities and food supplies in fringe areas will be most serious in their effect. Now, how do we stop them?"

Amberley of Science could only say, "Finding ten men in two hundred and twenty million is an awfully small needle in an awfully large haystack."

Jeffreys shook his head. "You have it wrong. Ten humanoids among two hundred twenty million humans."

"No difference," said Amberley of Science. "We don't know that a humanoid can be differentiated from a human at sight. Probably not." He looked at Lynn. They all did.

Lynn said heavily, "We in Cheyenne couldn't make one that would pass as human in the daylight."

"But They can," said Macalaster of Security, "and not only physically. We're sure of that. They've advanced mentalic procedures to the point where They can reel off the microelectronic pattern of the brain and focus it on the positronic pathways of the robot."

Lynn stared. "Are you implying that They can create the replica of a human being complete with personality and memory?"

"I am."

"Of specific human beings?"

"That's right."

"Is this also based on Agent Breckenridge's findings?"

"Yes. The evidence can't be disputed."

Lynn bent his head in thought for a moment. Then he said, "Then ten men in the United States are not men but humanoids. But the originals would have had to be available to them. They couldn't be Orientals, who would be too easy to spot, so they would have to be East Europeans. How would they be introduced into this country, then? With the radar network over the entire world border as tight as a drum, how could They introduce any individual, human or humanoid, without our knowing it?"

Macalaster of Security said, "It can be done. There are certain legitimate seepages across the border. Businessmen, pilots, even tourists. They're watched, of course, on both sides. Still ten of them might have been kidnapped and used as models for humanoids. The humanoids would then be sent back in their place. Since we wouldn't expect such a substitution, it would pass us by. If they were Americans to begin with, there would be no difficulty in their getting into this country. It's as simple as that."

"And even their friends and family could not tell the difference?"

"We must assume so. Believe me, we've been waiting for any report that might imply sudden attacks of amnesia or troublesome changes in personality. We've checked on thousands."

Amberley of Science stared at his finger tips. "I think ordinary measures won't work. The attack must come from the Bureau of Robotics and I depend on the chief of that bureau."

Again eyes turned sharply, expectantly, on Lynn.

Lynn felt bitterness rise. It seemed to him that this was what the conference came to and was intended for. Nothing that had been said had not been said before. He was sure of that. There was no solution to the problem, no pregnant suggestion. It was a device for the record, a device on the part of men who gravely feared defeat and who wished the responsibility for it placed clearly and unequivocally on someone else.

And yet there was justice in it. It was in robotics that We had fallen short. And Lynn was not Lynn merely. He was Lynn of Robotics and the responsibility had to be his.

He said, "I will do what I can."

He spent a wakeful night and there was a haggardness about both body and soul when he sought and attained another interview with Presidential Assistant Jeffreys the next morning. Breckenridge was there, and though Lynn would have preferred a private conference, he could see the justice in the situation. It was obvious that Breckenridge had attained enormous influence with the government as a result of his successful Intelligence work. Well, why not?

Lynn said, "Sir, I am considering the possibility that we are hopping uselessly to enemy piping."

"In what way?"

"I'm sure that however impatient the public may grow at times, and however legislators sometimes find it expedient to talk, the government at least recognizes the world stalemate to be beneficial. They must recognize it also. Ten humanoids with one TC bomb is a trivial way of breaking the stalemate."

"The destruction of fifteen million human beings is scarcely trivial."

"It is from the world power standpoint. It would not so demoralize us as to make us surrender or so cripple us as to convince us we could not win. There would just be the same old planetary death war that both sides have avoided so long and so successfully. And all They would have accomplished is to force us to fight minus one city. It's not enough."

"What do you suggest?" said Jeffreys coldly. "That They do not have ten humanoids in our country? That there is not a TC bomb waiting to get together?"

"I'll agree that those things are here, but perhaps for some reason greater than just midwinter bomb madness."

"Such as?"

"It may be that the physical destruction resulting from the humanoids getting together is not the worst thing that can happen to us. What about the moral and intellectual destruction that comes of their being here at all? With all due respect to Agent Breckenridge, what if They *intended* for us to find out about the humanoids; what if the humanoids are never supposed to get together, but merely to remain separate in order to give us something to worry about?"

"Why?"

"Tell me this. What measures have already been taken against the humanoids? I suppose that Security is going through the files of all citizens who have ever been across the border or close enough to it to make kidnaping possible. I know, since Macalaster mentioned it yesterday, that they are following up suspicious psychiatric cases. What else?"

Jeffreys said, "Small X-ray devices are being installed in key places in the large cities. In the mass arenas, for instance—"

"Where ten humanoids might slip in among a hundred thousand spectators of a football game or an air-polo match?"

"Exactly."

"And concert halls and churches?"

"We must start somewhere. We can't do it all at once."

"Particularly when panic must be avoided," said Lynn. "Isn't that so? It wouldn't do to have the public realize that at any unpredictable moment, some unpredictable city and its human contents would suddenly cease to exist."

"I suppose that's obvious. What are you driving at?"

Lynn said strenuously, "That a growing fraction of our national effort will be diverted entirely into the nasty problem of what Amberley called finding a very small needle in a very large haystack. We'll be chasing our tails madly, while They increase their research lead to the point where we find we can no longer catch up; when we must surrender without the chance even of snapping our fingers in retaliation.

"Consider further that this news will leak out as more and more people become involved in our countermeasures and more and more people begin to guess what we're doing. Then what? The panic might do us more harm than any one TC bomb."

The Presidential Assistant said irritably, "In Heaven's name, man, what do you suggest we do, then?"

"Nothing," said Lynn. "Call their bluff. Live as we have lived and gamble that They won't dare break the stalemate for the sake of a one-bomb head start."

"Impossible!" said Jeffreys. "Completely impossible. The welfare of all of Us is very largely in my hands, and doing nothing is the one thing I cannot do. I agree with you, perhaps, that X-ray machines at sports arenas are a kind of skin-deep measure that won't be effective, but it has to be done so that people, in the aftermath, do not come to the bitter conclusion that we tossed our country away for the sake of a subtle line of reasoning that encouraged donothingism. In fact, our countergambit will be active indeed."

"In what way?"

Presidential Assistant Jeffreys looked at Breckenridge. The young Security officer, hitherto calmly silent, said, "It's no use talking about a possible future break in the stalemate when the stalemate is broken now. It doesn't matter whether these humanoids explode or do not. Maybe they *are* only a bait to divert us, as you say. But the fact remains that we are a quarter of a century behind in robotics, and that may be fatal. What other advances in robotics will there be to surprise us if war does start? The only answer is to divert our entire force immediately, *now*, into a crash program of robotics research, and the first problem is to find the humanoids. Call it an exercise in robotics, if you will, or call it the prevention of the death of fifteen million men, women and children."

Lynn shook his head helplessly. "You *can't*. You'd be playing into their hands. They want us lured into the one blind alley while they're free to advance in all other directions."

Jeffreys said impatiently, "That's your guess. Breckenridge has made his suggestion through channels and the government has approved, and we will begin with an all-Science conference."

"All-Science?"

Breckenridge said, "We have listed every important scientist of every branch of natural science. They'll all be at Cheyenne. There will be only one point on the agenda: How to advance robotics. The major specific subheading under that will be: How to develop a receiving device for the electromagnetic fields of the cerebral cortex that will be sufficiently delicate to distinguish between a protoplasmic human brain and a positronic humanoid brain."

Jeffreys said, "We had hoped you would be willing to be in charge of the conference."

"I was not consulted in this."

"Obviously time was short, sir. Do you agree to be in charge?"

Lynn smiled briefly. It was a matter of responsibility again. The responsibility must be clearly that of Lynn of Robotics. He had the feeling it would be Breckenridge who would really be in charge. But what could he do?

He said, "I agree."

Breckenridge and Lynn returned together to Cheyenne, where that evening Laszlo listened with a sullen mistrust to Lynn's description of coming events.

Laszlo said, "While you were gone, Chief, I've started putting five experimental models of humanoid structure through the testing procedures. Our men are on a twelve-hour day, with three shifts overlapping. If we've got to arrange a conference, we're going to be crowded and red-taped out of everything. Work will come to a halt."

Breckenridge said, "That will be only temporary. You will gain more than you lose."

Laszlo scowled. "A bunch of astrophysicists and geochemists around won't help a damn toward robotics."

"Views from specialists of other fields may be helpful."

"Are you sure? How do we know that there *is* any way of detecting brain waves or that, even if we can, there is a way of differentiating human and humanoid by wave pattern? Who set up the project, anyway?"

"I did," said Breckenridge.

"You did? Are you a robotics man?"

The young Security agent said calmly, "I have studied robotics."

"That's not the same thing."

"I've had access to text material dealing with Russian robotics—in Russian. Top-secret material well in advance of anything you have here."

Lynn said ruefully, "He has us there, Laszlo."

"It was on the basis of that material," Breckenridge went on, "that I suggested this particular line of investigation. It is reasonably certain that in copying off the electromagnetic pattern of a specific human mind into a specific positronic brain, a perfectly exact duplicate cannot be made. For one thing, the most complicated positronic brain small enough to fit into a human-sized skull is hundreds of times less complex than the human brain. It can't pick up all the overtones, therefore, and there must be some way to take advantage of that fact."

Laszlo looked impressed despite himself and Lynn smiled grimly. It was easy to resent Breckenridge and the coming intrusion of several hundred scientists of nonrobotics specialties, but the problem itself was an intriguing one. There was that consolation, at least.

It came to him quietly.

Lynn found he had had nothing to do but sit in his office alone, with an executive position that had grown merely titular. Perhaps that helped. It gave him time to think, to picture the creative scientists of half the world converging on Cheyenne.

It was Breckenridge, who, with cool efficiency, was handling the details of preparation. There had been a kind of confidence in the way he said, "Let's get together and we'll lick Them."

Let's get together.

It came to Lynn so quietly that anyone watching Lynn at that moment might have seen his eyes blink twice—but surely nothing more.

He did what he had to do with a whirling detachment that kept him calm when he felt that, by all rights, he ought to be going mad.

He sought out Breckenridge in the other's improvised quarters. Breckenridge was alone and frowning. "Is anything wrong, sir?"

Lynn said wearily, "Everything's right, I think. I've invoked martial law."

"What!"

"As chief of a division I can do so if I am of the opinion the situation warrants it. Over my division I can then be dictator. Chalk up one for the beauties of decentralization."

"You will rescind that order immediately." Breckenridge took a step forward. "When Washington hears this, you will be ruined."

"I'm ruined anyway. Do you think I don't realize that I've been set up for the role of the greatest villain in American history: the man who let Them break the stalemate? I have nothing to lose—and perhaps a great deal to gain."

He laughed a little wildly. "What a target the Division of Robotics will be, eh, Breckenridge? Only a few thousand men to be killed by a TC bomb capable of wiping out three hundred square miles in one micro-second. But five hundred of those men would be our greatest scientists. We would be in the peculiar position of having to fight a war with our brains shot out, or surrendering. I think we'd surrender."

"But this is impossible. Lynn, do you hear me? Do you understand? How could the humanoids pass our security provisions? How could they get together?"

"But they *are* getting together! We're helping them to do so. We're ordering them to do so. Our scientists visit the other side, Breckenridge. They visit Them regularly. You made a point of how strange it was that no one in robotics did. Well, ten of those scientists are still there in their place, ten humanoids are converging on Cheyenne."

"That's a ridiculous guess."

"I think it's a good one, Breckenridge. But it wouldn't work unless we knew humanoids were in America so that we would

call the conference in the first place. Quite a coincidence that
you brought the news of the humanoids *and* suggested the
conference *and* suggested the agenda *and* are running the show
and know exactly which scientists were invited. Did you make
sure the right ten were included?"

"Dr. Lynn!" cried Breckenridge in outrage. He poised to
rush forward.

Lynn said, "Don't move. I've got a blaster here. We'll just
wait for the scientists to get here one by one. One by one we'll
X-ray them. One by one, we'll monitor them for radioactivity.
No two will get together without being checked, and if all five
hundred are clear, I'll give you my blaster and surrender to
you. Only I think we'll find the ten humanoids. Sit down,
Breckenridge."

They both sat.

Lynn said, "We wait. When I'm tired, Laszlo will spell me.
We wait."

Professor Manuelo Jiminez of the Institute of Higher Studies
of Buenos Aires exploded while the stratospheric jet on which
he traveled was three miles above the Amazon Valley. It was
a simple chemical explosion but it was enough to destroy the
plane.

Dr. Herman Liebowitz of M. I. T. exploded in a mono-rail,
killing twenty people and injuring a hundred others.

In similar manner, Dr. Auguste Marin of L'Institut Nu-
cléonique of Montreal and seven others died at various stages
of their journey to Cheyenne.

Laszlo hurtled in, pale-faced and stammering, with the first
news of it. It had only been two hours that Lynn had sat there,
facing Breckenridge, blaster in hand.

Laszlo said, "I thought you were nuts, Chief, but you were
right. They *were* humanoids. They *had* to be." He turned to
stare with hate-filled eyes at Breckenridge. "Only they were
warned. *He* warned them, and now there won't be one left
intact. Not one to study."

"God!" cried Lynn and in a frenzy of haste thrust his blaster
out toward Breckenridge and fired. The Security man's neck
vanished; the torso fell; the head dropped, thudded against the
floor and rolled crookedly.

Lynn moaned, "I didn't understand, I thought he was a
traitor. Nothing more."

And Laszlo stood immobile, mouth open, for the moment incapable of speech.

Lynn said wildly, "Sure, he warned them. But how could he do so while sitting in that chair unless he were equipped with built-in radio transmission? Don't you see it? Breckenridge had been in Moscow. The real Breckenridge is still there. Oh my God, there were *eleven* of them."

Laszlo managed a hoarse squeak. "Why didn't *he* explode?"

"He was hanging on, I suppose, to make sure the others had received his message and were safely destroyed. Lord, Lord, when you brought the news and I realized the truth, I couldn't shoot fast enough. God knows by how few seconds I may have beaten him to it."

Laszlo said shakily, "At least, we'll have one to study." He bent and put his fingers on the sticky fluid trickling out of the mangled remains at the neck end of the headless body.

Not blood, but high-grade machine oil.

PART III

Susan Calvin

Satisfaction Guaranteed

The robot short stories that most interested me, however, were those that dealt with Dr. Susan Calvin, robopsychologist extraordinary. A "robopsychologist" is not a robot who is a psychologist, but a psychologist who is also a roboticist. It is an ambiguous word, unfortunately, but I am stuck with it.

As time went on, I fell in love with Dr. Calvin. She was a forbidding creature, to be sure—much more like the popular conception of a robot than were any of my positronic creations—but I loved her anyway.

She served as the central bond that knit together the stories of I, Robot, and in four of the stories she played a central role. What's more, after I, Robot appeared (and despite the fact that the book contained an epilog briefly noting Dr. Calvin's death at an advanced age) I couldn't help bringing her back. I wrote four more stories dealing with her.

In one of these, dear Susan appeared only glancingly. This was "Satisfaction Guaranteed," which appeared in the April 1951 issue of Amazing Stories.

An interesting point about this story is the unusual quantity of mail from readers, almost all young ladies, and almost all speaking wistfully of Tony—as though I might know where he could be found.

I shall attempt to draw no morals (or immorals, either) from this.

Satisfaction Guaranteed

Tony was tall and darkly handsome, with an incredibly patrician air drawn into every line of his unchangeable expression, and Claire Belmont regarded him through the crack in the door with a mixture of horror and dismay.

"I can't, Larry. I just can't have him in the house." Feverishly, she was searching her paralyzed mind for a stronger way of putting it; some way that would make sense and settle things, but she could only end with a simple repetition.

"Well, I can't!"

Larry Belmont regarded his wife stiffly, and there was that spark of impatience in his eyes that Claire hated to see, since she felt her own incompetence mirrored in it. "We're committed, Claire," he said, "and I can't have you backing out now. The company is sending me to Washington on this basis, and it probably means a promotion. It's perfectly safe and you know it. What's your objection?"

She frowned helplessly. "It just gives me the chills. I couldn't bear him."

"He's as human as you or I, almost. So, no nonsense. Come, get out there."

His hand was in the small of her back, shoving; and she found herself in her own living room, shivering. *It* was there, looking at her with a precise politeness, as though appraising his hostess-to-be of the next three weeks. Dr. Susan Calvin was there, too, sitting stiffly in thin-lipped abstraction. She had the cold, faraway look of someone who has worked with machines so long that a little of the steel had entered the blood.

"Hello," crackled Claire in general, and ineffectual, greeting.

But Larry was busily saving the situation with a spurious gaiety. "Here, Claire, I want you to meet Tony, a swell guy. This is my wife, Claire, Tony, old boy." Larry's hand draped itself amiably over Tony's shoulder, but Tony remained unresponsive and expressionless under the pressure.

He said, "How do you do, Mrs. Belmont."

And Claire jumped at Tony's voice. It was deep and mellow, smooth as the hair on his head or the skin on his face.

Before she could stop herself, she said, "Oh, my—you talk."

"Why not? Did you expect that I didn't?"

But Claire could only smile weakly. She didn't really know what she had expected. She looked away, then let him slide gently into the corner of her eye. His hair was smooth and black, like polished plastic—or was it really composed of separate hairs? And was the even, olive skin of his hands and face continued on past the obscurement of his formally cut clothing?

She was lost in the shuddering wonder of it, and had to force her thoughts back into place to meet Dr. Calvin's flat, unemotional voice.

"Mrs. Belmont, I hope you appreciate the importance of this experiment. Your husband tells me he has given you some of the background. I would like to give you more, as the senior psychologist of the U. S. Robots and Mechanical Men Corporation.

"Tony is a robot. His actual designation on the company files is TN-3, but he will answer to Tony. He is not a mechanical monster nor simply a calculating machine of the type that were developed during World War II, fifty years ago. He has an artificial brain nearly as complicated as our own. It is an immense telephone switchboard on an atomic scale, so that billions of possible 'telephone connections' can be compressed into an instrument that will fit inside a skull.

"Such brains are manufactured for each model of robot specifically. Each contains a precalculated set of connections so that each robot knows the English language to start with and enough of anything else that may be necessary to perform his job.

"Until now, U. S. Robots has confined its manufacturing activity to industrial models for use in places where human labor is impractical—in deep mines, for instance, or in underwater work. But we want to invade the city and the home. To do so, we must get the ordinary man and woman to accept these robots without fear. You understand that there is nothing to fear."

"There isn't, Claire," interposed Larry earnestly. "Take my word for it. It's impossible for him to do any harm. You know I wouldn't leave him with you otherwise."

Claire cast a quick, secret glance at Tony and lowered her voice. "What if I make him angry?"

"You needn't whisper," said Dr. Calvin calmly. "He *can't* get angry with you, my dear. I told you that the switchboard connections of his brain were predetermined. Well, the most important connection of all is what we call 'The First Law of Robotics,' and it is merely this: 'No robot can harm a human being, or, through inaction, allow a human being to come to harm.' All robots are built so. No robot can be forced in any way to do harm to any human. So, you see, we need you and Tony as a preliminary experiment for our own guidance, while your husband is in Washington to arrange for government supervised legal tests."

"You mean all this isn't legal?"

Larry cleared his throat. "Not just yet, but it's all right. He won't leave the house, and you mustn't let anyone see him. That's all. . . . And, Claire, I'd stay with you, but I know too much about the robots. We must have a completely inexperienced tester so that we can have severe conditions. It's necessary."

"Oh, well," muttered Claire. Then, as a thought struck her, "But what does he do?"

"Housework," said Dr. Calvin shortly.

She got up to leave, and it was Larry who saw her to the

front door. Claire stayed behind drearily. She caught a glimpse of herself in the mirror above the mantelpiece, and looked away hastily. She was very tired of her small, mousy face and her dim, unimaginative hair. Then she caught Tony's eyes upon her and almost smiled before she remembered. . . .

He was only a machine.

Larry Belmont was on his way to the airport when he caught a glimpse of Gladys Claffern. She was the type of woman who seemed made to be seen in glimpses. . . . Perfectly and precisely manufactured; dressed with thoughtful hand and eye; too gleaming to be stared at.

The little smile that preceded her and the faint scent that trailed her were a pair of beckoning fingers. Larry felt his stride break; he touched his hat, then hurried on.

As always he felt that vague anger. If Claire could only push her way into the Claffern clique, it would help so much. But what was the use.

Claire! The few times she had come face to face with Gladys, the little fool had been tongue-tied. He had no illusions. The testing of Tony was his big chance, and it was in Claire's hands. How much safer it would be in the hands of someone like Gladys Claffern.

Claire woke the second morning to the sound of a subdued knock on the bedroom door. Her mind clamored, then went icy. She had avoided Tony the first day, smiling thinly when she met him and brushing past with a wordless sound of apology.

"Is that you—Tony?"

"Yes, Mrs. Belmont. May I enter?"

She must have said yes, because he was in the room, quite suddenly and noiselessly. Her eyes and nose were simultaneously aware of the tray he was carrying.

"Breakfast?" she said.

"If you please."

She wouldn't have dared to refuse, so she pushed herself slowly into a sitting position and received it: poached eggs, buttered toast, coffee.

"I have brought the sugar and cream separately," said Tony. "I expect to learn your preference with time, in this and in other things."

She waited.

Tony, standing there straight and pliant as a metal rule, asked, after a moment, "Would you prefer to eat in privacy?"

"Yes. . . . I mean, if you don't mind."

"Will you need help later in dressing?"

"Oh, my, no!" She clutched frantically at the sheet, so that the coffee hovered at the edge of catastrophe. She remained so, in rigor, then sank helplessly back against the pillow when the door closed him out of her sight again.

She got through breakfast somehow. . . . He was only a machine, and if it were only more visible that he were it wouldn't be so frightening. Or if his expression would change. It just stayed there, nailed on. You couldn't tell what went on behind those dark eyes and that smooth, olive skin-stuff. The coffee cup beat a faint castanet for a moment as she set it back, on the tray.

Then she realized that she had forgotten to add the sugar and cream after all, and she did so hate black coffee.

She burned a straight path from bedroom to kitchen after dressing. It was her house, after all, and there wasn't anything frippy about her, but she liked her kitchen clean. He should have waited for supervision. . . .

But when she entered, she found a kitchen that might have been minted fire-new from the factory the moment before.

She stopped, stared, turned on her heel and nearly ran into Tony. She yelped.

"May I help?" he asked.

"Tony," and she scraped the anger off the edges of her mind's panic, "you must make some noise when you walk. I can't have you stalking me, you know. . . . Didn't you use this kitchen?"

"I did, Mrs. Belmont."

"It doesn't look it."

"I cleaned up afterward. Isn't that customary?"

Claire opened her eyes wide. After all, what could one say to that. She opened the oven compartment that held the pots, took a quick, unseeing look at the metallic glitter inside, then said with a tremor, "Very good. Quite satisfactory."

If at the moment, he had beamed; if he had smiled; if he had quirked the corner of his mouth the slightest bit, she felt that she could have warmed to him. But he remained an English lord in repose, as he said, "Thank you, Mrs. Belmont. Would you come into the living room?"

She did, and it struck her at once. "Have you been polishing the furniture?"

"Is it satisfactory, Mrs. Belmont?"

"But when? You didn't do it yesterday."

"Last night, of course."

"You burned the lights all night?"

"Oh, no. That wouldn't have been necessary. I've a built-in ultraviolet source. I can see in ultraviolet. And, of course, I don't require sleep."

He did require admiration, though. She realized that, then. He had to know that he was pleasing her. But she couldn't bring herself to supply that pleasure for him.

She could only say sourly, "Your kind will put ordinary houseworkers out of business."

"There is work of much greater importance they can be put to in the world, once they are freed of drudgery. After all, Mrs. Belmont, things like myself can be manufactured. But nothing yet can imitate the creativity and versatility of a human brain, like yours."

And though his face gave no hint, his voice was warmly surcharged with awe and admiration, so that Claire flushed and muttered, "My brain! You can have it."

Tony approached a little and said, "You must be unhappy to say such a thing. Is there anything I can do?"

For a moment, Claire felt like laughing. It *was* a ridiculous situation. Here was an animated carpet-sweeper, dishwasher, furniture-polisher, general factotum, rising from the factory table—and offering his services as consoler and confidant.

Yet she said suddenly, in a burst of woe and voice, "Mr. Belmont doesn't think I have a brain, if you must know. . . . And I suppose I haven't." She couldn't cry in front of him. She felt, for some reason, that she had the honor of the human race to support against this mere creation.

"It's lately," she added. "It was all right when he was a student; when he was just starting. But I can't be a big man's wife; and he's getting to be a big man. He wants me to be a hostess and an entry into social life for him—like G—guh—guh—Gladys Claffern."

Her nose was red, and she looked away.

But Tony wasn't watching her. His eyes wandered about the room. "I can help you run the house."

"But it's no good," she said fiercely. "It needs a touch I can't give it. I can only make it comfortable; I can't ever make it the kind they take pictures of for the Home Beautiful magazines."

"Do you want that kind?"

"Does it do any good—wanting?"

Tony's eyes were on her, full. "I could help."

"Do you know anything about interior decoration?"

"Is it something a good housekeeper should know?"

"Oh, yes."

"Then I have the potentialities of learning it. Can you get me books on the subject?"

Something started then.

Claire, clutching her hat against the brawling liberties of the wind, had manipulated two fat volumes on the home arts back from the public library. She watched Tony as he opened one of them and flipped the pages. It was the first time she had watched his fingers flicker at anything like fine work.

I don't see how they do it, she thought, and on a sudden impulse reached for his hand and pulled it toward herself. Tony did not resist, but let it lie limp for inspection.

She said, "It's remarkable. Even your fingernails look natural."

"That's deliberate, of course," said Tony. Then, chattily, "The skin is a flexible plastic, and the skeletal framework is a light metal alloy. Does that amuse you?"

"Oh, no." She lifted her reddened face. "I just feel a little embarrassed at sort of poking into your insides. It's none of my business. You don't ask me about mine."

"My brain paths don't include that type of curiosity. I can only act within my limitations, you know."

And Claire felt something tighten inside her in the silence that followed. Why did she keep forgetting he was a machine. Now the thing itself had to remind her. Was she so starved for sympathy that she would even accept a robot as equal—because he sympathized?

She noticed Tony was still flipping the pages—almost helplessly—and there was a quick, shooting sense of relieved superiority within her. "You can't read, can you?"

Tony looked up at her; his voice calm, unreproachful. "I *am* reading, Mrs. Belmont."

"But—" She pointed at the book in a meaningless gesture.

"I am scanning the pages, if that's what you mean. My sense of reading is photographic."

It was evening then, and when Claire eventually went to bed Tony was well into the second volume, sitting there in the dark, or what seemed dark to Claire's limited eyes.

Her last thought, the one that clamored at her just as her mind let go and tumbled, was a queer one. She remembered his hand again; the touch of it. It had been warm and soft, like a human being's.

How clever of the factory, she thought, and softly ebbed to sleep.

It was the library continuously, thereafter, for several days. Tony suggested the fields of study, which branched out quickly. There were books on color matching and on cosmetics; on carpentry and on fashions; on art and on the history of costumes.

He turned the pages of each book before his solemn eyes, and, as quickly as he turned, he read; nor did he seem capable of forgetting.

Before the end of the week, he had insisted on cutting her hair, introducing her to a new method of arranging it, adjusting her eyebrow line a bit and changing the shade of her powder and lipstick.

She had palpitated in nervous dread for half an hour under the delicate touch of his inhuman fingers and then looked in the mirror.

"There is more that can be done," said Tony, "especially in clothes. How do you find it for a beginning?"

And she hadn't answered; not for quite a while. Not until she had absorbed the identity of the stranger in the glass and cooled the wonder at the beauty of it all. Then she had said chokingly, never once taking her eyes from the warming image, "Yes, Tony, quite good—for a beginning."

She said nothing of this in her letters to Larry. Let him see it all at once. And something in her realized that it wasn't only the surprise she would enjoy. It was going to be a kind of revenge.

Tony said one morning, "It's time to start buying, and I'm not allowed to leave the house. If I write out exactly what we must have, can I trust you to get it? We need drapery, and furniture fabric, wallpaper, carpeting, paint, clothing—and any number of small things."

"You can't get these things to your own specifications at a stroke's notice," said Claire doubtfully.

"You can get fairly close, if you go through the city and if money is no object."

"But, Tony, money is certainly an object."

"Not at all. Stop off at U.S. Robots in the first place. I'll write a note for you. You see Dr. Calvin, and tell her that I said it was part of the experiment."

Dr. Calvin, somehow, didn't frighten her as on that first evening. with her new face and a new hat, she couldn't be quite the old Claire. The psychologist listened carefully, asked a few questions, nodded—and then Claire found herself walking out, armed with an unlimited charge account against the assets of U.S. Robots and Mechanical Men Corporation.

It is wonderful what money will do. With a store's contents at her feet, a saleslady's dictum was not necessarily a voice from above; the uplifted eyebrow of a decorator was not anything like Jove's thunder.

And once, when an Exalted Plumpness at one of the most lordly of the garment salons had insistently poohed her description of the wardrobe she must have with counter-pronouncements in accents of the purest Fifty-seventh Street French, she called up Tony, then held the phone out to Monsieur.

"If you don't mind"—voice firm, but fingers twisting a bit—"I'd like you to talk to my—uh—secretary."

Pudgy proceeded to the phone with a solemn arm crooked behind his back. He lifted the phone in two fingers and said delicately, "Yes." A short pause, another "Yes," then a much longer pause, a squeaky beginning of an objection that perished quickly, another pause, a very meek "Yes," and the phone was restored to its cradle.

"If Madam will come with me," he said, hurt and distant, "I will try to supply her needs."

"Just a second." Claire rushed back to the phone, and dialed

again. "Hello, Tony. I don't know what you said, but it worked.
Thanks. You're a—" She struggled for the appropriate word,
gave up and ended in a final little squeak, "—a—a dear!"

It was Gladys Claffern looking at her when she turned from
the phone again. A slightly amused and slightly amazed Gladys
Claffern, looking at her out of a face tilted a bit to one side.

"Mrs. Belmont?"

It all drained out of Claire—just like that. She could only
nod—stupidly, like a marionette.

Gladys smiled with an insolence you couldn't put your finger
on. "I didn't know you shopped here?" As if the place had, in
her eyes, definitely lost caste through the fact.

"I don't, usually," said Claire humbly.

"And haven't you done something to your hair? It's quite—
quaint. . . . Oh, I hope you'll excuse me, but isn't your husband's name Lawrence? It seems to me that it's Lawrence."

Claire's teeth clenched, but she had to explain. She *had* to.
"Tony is a friend of my husband's. He's helping me select
some things."

"I understand. And quite a *dear* about it, I imagine." She
passed on smiling, carrying the light and the warmth of the
world with her.

Claire did not question the fact that it was to Tony that she
turned for consolation. Ten days had cured her of reluctance.
And she could weep before him; weep and rage.

"I was a complete f-fool," she stormed, wrenching at her
waterlogged handkerchief. "She does that to me. I don't know
why. She just does. I should have—kicked her. I should have
knocked her down and stamped on her."

"Can you hate a human being so much?" asked Tony, in
puzzled softness. "That part of a human mind is closed to me."

"Oh, it isn't she," she moaned. "It's myself, I suppose.
She's everything I want to be—on the outside, anyway. . . . And I can't be."

Tony's voice was forceful and low in her ear. "You can be,
Mrs. Belmont. You *can* be. We have ten days yet, and in ten
days the house will no longer be itself. Haven't we been plan-
ning that?"

"And how will that help me—with her?"

"Invite her here. Invite her friends. Have it the evening

before I—before I leave. It will be a housewarming, in a way."

"She won't come."

"Yes, she will. She'll come to laugh.... And she won't be able to."

"Do you really think so? Oh, Tony, do you think we can do it?" She had both his hands in hers.... And then, with her face flung aside, "But what good would it be? It won't be I; it will be you that's doing it. I can't ride your back."

"Nobody lives in splendid singleness," whispered Tony. "They've put that knowledge in me. What you, or anyone, see in Gladys Claffern is not just Gladys Claffern. She rides the back of all that money and social position can bring. She doesn't question that. Why should you?... And look at it this way, Mrs. Belmont. I am manufactured to obey, but the extent of my obedience is for myself to determine. I can follow orders niggardly or liberally. For you, it is liberal, because you are what I have been manufactured to see human beings as. You are kind, friendly, unassuming. Mrs. Claffern, as you describe her, is not, and I wouldn't obey her as I would you. So it *is* you, and not I, Mrs. Belmont, that is doing all this."

He withdrew his hands from hers then, and Claire looked at that expressionless face no one could read—wondering. She was suddenly frightened again in a completely new way.

She swallowed nervously and stared at her hands, which were still tingling with the pressure of his fingers. She hadn't imagined it; his fingers had pressed hers, gently, tenderly, just before they moved away.

No!

Its fingers... *Its* fingers....

She ran to the bathroom and scrubbed her hands—blindly, uselessly.

She was a bit shy of him the next day; watching him narrowly; waiting to see what might follow—and for a while nothing did.

Tony was working. If there was any difficulty in technique in putting up wallpaper, or utilizing the quick-drying paint, Tony's activity did not show it. His hands moved precisely; his fingers were deft and sure.

He worked all night. She never heard him, but each morning was a new adventure. She couldn't count the number of things that had been done, and by evening she was still finding new touches—and another night had come.

She tried to help only once and her human clumsiness marred that. *He* was in the next room, and she was hanging a picture in the spot marked by Tony's mathematical eyes. The little mark was there; the picture was there; and a revulsion against idleness was there.

But she was nervous, or the ladder was rickety. It didn't matter. She felt it going, and she cried out. It tumbled without her, for Tony, with far more than flesh-and-blood quickness, had been under her.

His calm, dark eyes said nothing at all, and his warm voice said only words. "Are you hurt, Mrs. Belmont?"

She noticed for an instant that her falling hand must have mussed that sleek hair of his, because for the first time she could see for herself that it was composed of distinct strands— fine black hairs.

And then, all at once, she was conscious of his arms about her shoulders and under her knees—holding her tightly and warmly.

She pushed, and her scream was loud in her own ears. She spent the rest of the day in her room, and thereafter she slept with a chair upended against the doorknob of her bedroom door.

She had sent out the invitations, and, as Tony had said, they were accepted. She had only to wait for the last evening.

It came, too, after the rest of them, in its proper place. The house was scarcely her own. She went through it one last time—and every room had been changed. She, herself, was in clothes she would never have dared wear before. . . . And when you put them on, you put on pride and confidence with them.

She tried a polite look of contemptuous amusement before the mirror, and the mirror sneered back at her masterfully.

What would Larry say? . . . It didn't matter, somehow. The exciting days weren't coming with him. They were leaving with Tony. Now wasn't that strange? She tried to recapture her mood of three weeks before and failed completely.

The clock shrieked eight at her in eight breathless installments, and she turned to Tony. "They'll be here soon, Tony. You'd better get into the basement. We can't let them—"

She stared a moment, then said weakly, "Tony?" and more strongly, "Tony?" and nearly a scream, *"Tony!"*

But his arms were around her now; his face was close to hers; the pressure of his embrace was relentless. She heard his voice through a haze of emotional jumble.

"Claire," the voice said, "there are many things I am not made to understand, and this must be one of them. I am leaving tomorrow, and I don't want to. I find that there is more in me than just a desire to please you. Isn't it strange?"

His face was closer; his lips were warm, but with no breath behind them—for machines do not breathe. They were almost on hers.

. . . And the bell sounded.

For a moment, she struggled breathlessly, and then he was gone and nowhere in sight, and the bell was sounding again. Its intermittent shrillness was insistent.

The curtains on the front windows had been pulled open. They had been closed fifteen minutes earlier. She *knew* that.

They must have seen, then. They must *all* have seen—everything!

They came in so politely, all in a bunch—the pack come to howl—with their sharp, darting eyes piercing everywhere. They *had* seen. Why else would Gladys ask in her jabbingest manner after Larry? And Claire was spurred to a desperate and reckless defiance.

Yes, he *is* away. He'll be back tomorrow, I suppose. No, I haven't been lonely here myself. Not a bit. I've had an exciting time. And she laughed at them. Why not? What could they do? Larry would know the truth, if it ever came to him, the story of what they thought they saw.

But *they* didn't laugh.

She could read that in the fury in Gladys Claffern's eyes; in the false sparkle of her words; in her desire to leave early. And as she parted with them, she caught one last, anonymous whisper—disjointed.

". . . never saw anything like . . . so *handsome*—"

And she knew what it was that had enabled her to fingersnap them so. Let each cat mew; and let each cat know—that she might be prettier than Claire Belmont, and grander, and richer—but not one, *not one*, could have so handsome a lover!

And then she remembered again—again—again, that Tony was a machine, and her skin crawled.

"Go away! Leave me be!" she cried to the empty room and ran to her bed. She wept wakefully all that night and the next morning, almost before dawn, when the streets were empty, a car drew up to the house and took Tony away.

Lawrence Belmont passed Dr. Calvin's office, and, on impulse, knocked. He found her with Mathematician Peter Bogert, but did not hesitate on that account.

He said, "Claire tells me that U.S. Robots paid for all that was done at my house—"

"Yes," said Dr. Calvin. "We've written it off, as a valuable and necessary part of the experiment. With your new position as Associate Engineer, you'll be able to keep it up, I think."

"That's not what I'm worried about. With Washington agreeing to the test, we'll be able to get a TN model of our own by next year, I think." He turned hesitantly, as though to go, and as hesitantly turned back again.

"Well, Mr. Belmont?" asked Dr. Calvin, after a pause.

"I wonder—" began Larry. "I wonder what really happened there. She—Claire, I mean—seems so different. It's not just her looks—though, frankly, I'm amazed." He laughed nervously. "It's *her!* She's not my wife, really—I can't explain it."

"Why try? Are you disappointed with any part of the change?"

"On the contrary. But it's a little frightening, too, you see—"

"I wouldn't worry, Mr. Belmont. Your wife has handled herself very well. Frankly, I never expected to have the experiment yield such a thorough and complete test. We know exactly what corrections must be made in the TN model, and the credit belongs entirely to Mrs. Belmont. If you want me to be very honest, I think your wife deserves your promotion more than you do."

Larry flinched visibly at that. "As long as it's in the family," he murmured unconvincingly and left.

Susan Calvin looked after him, "I think that hurt—I hope . . . Have you read Tony's report, Peter?"

"Thoroughly," said Bogert. "And won't the TN-3 model need changes?"

"Oh, you think so, too?" questioned Calvin sharply. "What's your reasoning?"

Bogert frowned. "I don't need any. It's obvious on the face of it that we can't have a robot loose which makes love to his mistress, if you don't mind the pun."

"Love! Peter, you sicken me. You really don't understand? That machine had to obey the First Law. He couldn't allow harm to come to a human being, and harm was coming to Claire Belmont through her own sense of inadequacy. So he made love to her, since what woman would fail to appreciate the compliment of being able to stir passion in a machine—in a cold, soulless machine. And he opened the curtains that night deliberately, that the others might see and envy—without any risk possible to Claire's marriage. I think it was clever of Tony—"

"Do you? What's the difference whether it was pretense or not, Susan? It still has its horrifying effect. Read the report again. She avoided him. She screamed when he held her. She didn't sleep that last night—in hysterics. We can't have that."

"Peter, you're blind. You're as blind as I was. The TN model will be rebuilt entirely, but not for your reason. Quite otherwise; quite otherwise. Strange that I overlooked it in the first place," her eyes were opaquely thoughtful, "but perhaps it reflects a shortcoming in myself. You see, Peter, machines can't fall in love, but—even when it's hopeless and horrifying—women can!"

Risk

"Risk" appeared in the May 1955 issue of Astounding Science Fiction. Of my later robot stories, it was the most closely bound to I, Robot, for it was a sequel to "Little Lost Robot," one of the stories in that book. It involves a different robot and a different problem, but the same setting, the same human characters and the same research project.

Risk

Hyper Base had lived for this day. Spaced about the gallery of the viewing room, in order and precedence strictly dictated by protocol, was a group of officials, scientists, technicians and others who could only be lumped under the general classification of "personnel." In accordance with their separate temperaments they waited hopefully, uneasily, breathlessly, eagerly, or fearfully for this culmination of their efforts.

The hollowed interior of the asteroid known as Hyper Base had become for this day the center of a sphere of iron security that extended out for ten thousand miles. No ship might enter that sphere and live. No message might leave without scrutiny.

A hundred miles away, more or less, a small asteroid moved neatly in the orbit into which it had been urged a year before, an orbit that ringed Hyper Base in as perfect a circle as could be managed. The asteroidlet's identity number was H937, but no one on Hyper Base called it anything but It. ("Have you been out on it today?" "The general's on it, blowing his top," and eventually the impersonal pronoun achieved the dignity of capitalization.)

On It, unoccupied now as zero second approached, was the *Parsec*, the only ship of its kind ever built in the history of man. It lay, unmanned, ready for its takeoff into the inconceivable.

Gerald Black, who, as one of the bright young men in etherics engineering, rated a front-row view, cracked his large knuckles, then wiped his sweating palms on his stained white smock and said sourly, "Why don't you bother the general, or Her Ladyship there?"

Nigel Ronson, of Interplanetary Press, looked briefly across the gallery toward the glitter of Major General Richard Kallner and the unremarkable woman at his side, scarcely visible in the glare of his dress uniform. He said, "I would, except that I'm interested in news."

Ronson was short and plump. He painstakingly wore his hair in a quarter-inch bristle, his shirt collar open and his trouser leg ankle-short, in faithful imitation of the newsmen who were stock characters on TV shows. He was a capable reporter nevertheless.

Black was stocky, and his dark hairline left little room for forehead, but his mind was as keen as his strong fingers were blunt. He said, "They've got all the news."

"Nuts," said Ronson. "Kallner's got no body under that gold braid. Strip him and you'll find only a conveyer belt dribbling orders downward and shooting responsibility upward."

Black found himself at the point of a grin but squeezed it down. He said, "What about the Madam Doctor?"

"Dr. Susan Calvin of U.S. Robots and Mechanical Men, Incorporated," intoned the reporter. "The lady with hyperspace where her heart ought to be and liquid helium in her eyes. She'd pass through the sun and come out the other end encased in frozen flame."

Black came even closer to a grin. "How about Director Schloss, then?"

Ronson said glibly, "He knows too much. Between spending his time fanning the feeble flicker of intelligence in his listener and dimming his own brains for fear of blinding said listener permanently by sheer force of brilliance, he ends up saying nothing."

Black showed his teeth this time. "Now suppose you tell me why you pick on me."

"Easy, doctor. I looked at you and figured you're too ugly to be stupid and too smart to miss a possible opportunity at some good personal publicity."

"Remind me to knock you down someday," said Black. "What do you want to know?"

The man from Interplanetary Press pointed into the pit and said, "Is that thing going to work?"

Black looked downward too, and felt a vague chill riffle over him like the thin night wind of Mars. The pit was one large television screen, divided in two. One half was an overall view of It. On It's pitted gray surface was the *Parsec*, glowing mutedly in the feeble sunlight. The other half showed the control room of the *Parsec*. There was no life in that control room. In the pilot's seat was an object the vague humanity of which did not for a moment obscure the fact that it was only a positronic robot.

Black said, "Physically, mister, this will work. That robot will leave and come back. Space! how we succeeded with that part of it. I watched it all. I came here two weeks after I took my degree in etheric physics and I've been here, barring leave and furloughs, ever since. I was here when we sent the first piece of iron wire to Jupiter's orbit and back through hyperspace—and got back iron filings. I was here when we sent white mice there and back and ended up with mincemeat.

"We spent six months establishing an even hyperfield after that. We had to wipe out lags of as little as tenths of thousandths of seconds from point to point in matter being subjected to hypertravel. After that, the white mice started coming back intact. I remember when we celebrated for a week because one white mouse came back alive and lived ten minutes before dying. Now they live as long as we can take proper care of them."

Ronson said, "Great!"

Black looked at him obliquely. "I said, *physically* it will work. Those white mice that come back—"

"Well?"

"No minds. Not even little white mice-type minds. They won't eat. They have to be force-fed. They won't mate. They won't run. They sit. They sit. They sit. That's all. We finally worked up to sending a chimpanzee. It was pitiful. It was too close to a man to make watching it bearable. It came back a hunk of meat that could make crawling motions. It could move its eyes and sometimes it would scrabble. It whined and sat in its own wastes without the sense to move. Somebody shot it one day, and we were grateful for that. I tell you this, fella, nothing that ever went into hyperspace has come back with a mind."

"Is this for publication?"

"After this experiment, maybe. They expect great things of it." A corner of Black's mouth lifted.

"You don't?"

"With a robot at the controls? No." Almost automatically Black's mind went back to that interlude, some years back, in which he had been unwittingly responsible for the near loss of a robot. He thought of the Nestor robots that filled Hyper Base with smooth, ingrained knowledge and perfectionist shortcomings. What was the use of talking about robots? He was not, by nature, a missionary.

But then Ronson, filling the continuing silence with a bit of small talk, said, as he replaced the wad of gum in his mouth by a fresh piece, "Don't tell me *you're* anti-robot. I've always heard that scientists are the one group that aren't anti-robot."

Black's patience snapped. He said, "That's true, and that's the trouble. Technology's gone robot-happy. Any job has to have a robot, or the engineer in charge feels cheated. You want a doorstop; buy a robot with a thick foot. That's a serious thing." He was speaking in a low, intense voice, shoving the words directly into Ronson's ear.

Ronson managed to extricate his arm. He said, "Hey, I'm no robot. Don't take it out on me. I'm a man. *Homo sapiens.* You just broke an arm bone of mine. Isn't that proof?"

Having started, however, it took more than frivolity to stop Black. He said, "Do you know how much time was wasted on this setup? We've had a perfectly generalized robot built and we've given it one order. Period. I heard the order given. I've memorized it. Short and sweet. 'Seize the bar with a firm grip. Pull it toward you firmly. *Firmly!* Maintain your hold until the control board informs you that you have passed through hyperspace twice.'

"So at zero time, the robot will grab the control bar and pull it firmly toward himself. His hands are heated to blood temperature. Once the control bar is in position, heat expansion completes contact and hyperfield is initiated. If anything happens to his brain during the first trip through hyperspace, it doesn't matter. All he needs to do is maintain position one microinstant and the ship will come back and the hyperfield will flip off. Nothing can go wrong. Then we study all its generalized reactions and see what, if anything, has gone wrong."

Ronson looked blank. "This all makes sense to me."

"Does it?" asked Black bitterly. "And what will you learn from a robot brain? It's positronic, ours is cellular. It's metal, ours is protein. They're not the same. There's no comparison. Yet I'm convinced that on the basis of what they learn, or think they learn, from the robot, they'll send men into hyperspace. Poor devils!—Look, it's not a question of dying. It's coming back mindless. If you'd seen the chimpanzee, you'd know what I mean. Death is clean and final. The other thing—"

The reporter said, "Have you talked about this to anyone?"

Black said, "Yes. They say what you said. They say I'm anti-robot and that settles everything.—Look at Susan Calvin there. You can bet *she* isn't anti-robot. She came all the way from Earth to watch this experiment. If it had been a man at the controls, she wouldn't have bothered. But what's the use!"

"Hey," said Ronson, "don't stop now. There's more."

"More what?"

"More problems. You've explained the robot. But why the security provisions all of a sudden?"

"Huh?"

"Come *on*. Suddenly I can't send dispatches. Suddenly ships can't come into the area. What's going on? This is just another experiment. The public knows about hyperspace and what you boys are trying to do, so what's the big secret?"

The backwash of anger was still seeping over Black, anger against the robots, anger against Susan Calvin, anger at the memory of that little lost robot in his past. There was some to spare, he found, for the irritating little newsman and his irritating little questions.

He said to himself, Let's see how he takes it.

He said, "You really want to know?"

"You bet."

"All right. We've never initiated a hyperfield for any object a millionth as large as that ship, or to send anything a millionth as far. That means that the hyperfield that will soon be initiated is some million million times as energetic as any we've ever handled. We're not sure what it can do."

"What do you mean?"

"Theory tells us that the ship will be neatly deposited out near Sirius and neatly brought back here. But how large a volume of space about the *Parsec* will be carried with it? It's hard to tell. We don't know enough about hyperspace. The asteroid on which the ship sits may go with it and, you know, if our calculations are even a little off, it may never be brought back here. It may return, say, twenty billion miles away. And there's a chance that more of space than just the asteroid may be shifted."

"How much more?" demanded Ronson.

"We can't say. There's an element of statistical uncertainty. That's why no ships must approach too closely. That's why we're keeping things quiet till the experiment is safely over."

Ronson swallowed audibly. "Supposing it reaches to Hyper Base?"

"There's a chance of it," said Black with composure. "Not much of a chance or Director Schloss wouldn't be here, I assure you. Still, there's a mathematical chance."

The newsman looked at his watch. "When does this all happen?"

"In about five minutes. You're not nervous, are you?"

"No," said Ronson, but he sat down blankly and asked no more questions.

Black leaned outward over the railing. The final minutes were ticking off.

The robot moved!

There was a mass sway of humanity forward at that sign of motion and the lights dimmed in order to sharpen and heighten the brightness of the scene below. But so far it was only the first motion. The hands of the robot approached the starting bar.

Black waited for the final second when the robot would pull the bar toward himself. Black could imagine a number of possibilities, and all sprang nearly simultaneously to mind.

There would first be the short flicker that would indicate the departure through hyperspace and return. Even though the time interval was exceedingly short, return would not be to the *precise* starting position and there would be a flicker. There always was.

Then, when the ship returned, it might be found, perhaps, that the devices to even the field over the huge volume of the ship had proved inadequate. The robot might be scrap steel. The ship might be scrap steel.

Or their calculations might be somewhat off and the ship might never return. Or worse still, Hyper Base might go with the ship and never return.

Or, of course, all might be well. The ship might flicker and be there in perfect shape. The robot, with mind untouched, would get out of his seat and signal a successful completion of the first voyage of a man-made object beyond the gravitational control of the sun.

The last minute was ticking off.

The last second came and the robot seized the starting bar and pulled it firmly toward himself—

Nothing!

No flicker. Nothing!

The *Parsec* never left normal space.

Major General Kallner took off his officer's cap to mop his glistening forehead and in doing so exposed a bald head that would have aged him ten years in appearance if his drawn expression had not already done so. Nearly an hour had passed since the *Parsec's* failure and nothing had been done.

"How did it happen? How did it happen? I don't understand it."

Dr. Mayer Schloss, who at forty was the "grand old man" of the young science of hyperfield matrices, said hopelessly, "There is nothing wrong with the basic theory. I'll swear my life away on that. There's a mechanical failure on the ship somewhere. Nothing more." He had said that a dozen times.

"I thought everything was tested." That had been said too.

"It was, sir, it was. Just the same—" And that.

They sat staring at each other in Kallner's office, which was now out of bounds for all personnel. Neither quite dared to look at the third person present.

Susan Calvin's thin lips and pale cheeks bore no expression. She said coolly, "You may console yourself with what I have told you before. It is doubtful whether anything useful would have resulted."

"This is not the time for the old argument," groaned Schloss.

"I am not arguing. U.S. Robots and Mechanical Men, Inc. will supply robots made up to specification to any legal purchaser for any legal use. We did our part, however. We informed you that we could not guarantee being able to draw conclusions with regard to the human brain from anything that happened to the positronic brain. Our responsibility ends there. There is no argument."

"Great space," said General Kallner, in a tone that made the expletive feeble indeed. "Let's not discuss that."

"What else was there to do?" muttered Schloss, driven to the subject nevertheless. "Until we know exactly what's happening to the mind in hyperspace we can't progress. The robot's mind is at least capable of mathematical analysis. It's a start, a beginning. And until we try—" He looked up wildly, "But your robot isn't the point, Dr. Calvin. We're not worried about him or his positronic brain. Damn it, woman—" His voice rose nearly to a scream.

The robopsychologist cut him to silence with a voice that scarcely raised itself from its level monotone. "No hysteria, man. In my lifetime I have witnessed many crises and I have never seen one solved by hysteria. I want answers to some questions."

Schloss's full lips trembled and his deep-set eyes seemed to retreat into their sockets and leave pits of shadow in their places. He said harshly, "Are you trained in etheric engineering?"

"That is an irrelevant question. I am Chief Robopsychologist of the United States Robots and Mechanical Men, Incorporated. That is a positronic robot sitting at the controls of the *Parsec*. Like all such robots, it is leased and not sold. I have a right to demand information concerning any experiment in which such a robot is involved."

"Talk to her, Schloss," barked General Kallner. "She's—she's all right."

Dr. Calvin turned her pale eyes on the general, who had been present at the time of the affair of the lost robot and who therefore could be expected not to make the mistake of underestimating her. (Schloss had been out on sick leave at the time, and hearsay is not as effective as personal experience.) "Thank you, general," she said.

Schloss looked helplessly from one to the other and muttered, "What do you want to know?"

"Obviously my first question is, What *is* your problem if the robot is not?"

"But the problem is an obvious one. The ship hasn't moved. Can't you see that? Are you blind?"

"I see quite well. What I don't see is your obvious panic over some mechanical failure. Don't you people expect failure sometimes?"

The general muttered, "It's the expense. The ship was hellishly expensive. The World Congress—appropriations—" He bogged down.

"The ship's still there. A slight overhaul and correction would involve no great trouble."

Schloss had taken hold of himself. The expression on his face was one of a man who had caught his soul in both hands, shaken it hard and set it on its feet. His voice had even achieved a kind of patience. "Dr. Calvin, when I say a mechanical failure, I mean something like a relay jammed by a speck of dust, a connection inhibited by a spot of grease, a transistor balked by a momentary heat expansion. A dozen other things. A hundred other things. Any of them can be quite temporary. They can stop taking effect at any moment."

"Which means that at any moment the *Parsec* may flash through hyperspace and back after all."

"Exactly. Now do you understand?"

"Not at all. Wouldn't that be just what you want?"

Schloss made a motion that looked like the start of an effort to seize a double handful of hair and yank. He said, "You are not an etherics engineer."

"Does that tongue-tie you, doctor?"

"We had the ship set," said Schloss despairingly, "to make a jump from a definite point in space relative to the center of gravity of the galaxy to another point. The return was to be to the original point corrected for the motion of the solar system. In the hour that has passed since the *Parsec* should have moved, the solar system has shifted position. The original parameters to which the hyperfield is adjusted no longer apply. The ordinary laws of motion do not apply to hyperspace and it would take us a week of computation to calculate a new set of parameters."

"You mean that if the ship moves now it will return to some unpredictable point thousands of miles away?"

"Unpredictable?" Schloss smiled hollowly. "Yes, I should

call it that. The *Parsec* might end up in the Andromeda nebula or in the center of the sun. In any case the odds are against our even seeing it again."

Susan Calvin nodded. "The situation then is that if the ship disappears, as it may do at any moment, a few billion dollars of the taxpayers' money may be irretrievably gone, and—it will be said—through bungling."

Major General Kallner could not have winced more noticeably if he had been poked with a sharp pin in the fundament.

The robopsychologist went on, "Somehow, then, the ship's hyperfield mechanism must be put out of action, and that as soon as possible. Something will have to be unplugged or jerked loose or flicked off." She was speaking half to herself.

"It's not that simple," said Schloss. "I can't explain it completely, since you're not an etherics expert. It's like trying to break an ordinary electric circuit by slicing through high-tension wire with garden shears. It could be disastrous. It *would* be disastrous."

"Do you mean that any attempt to shut off the mechanism would hurl the ship into hyperspace?"

"Any *random* attempt would *probably* do so. Hyper-forces are not limited by the speed of light. It is very probable that they have no limit of velocity at all. It makes things extremely difficult. The only reasonable solution is to discover the nature of the failure and learn from that a safe way of disconnecting the field."

"And how do you propose to do that, Dr. Schloss?"

Schloss said, "It seems to me that the only thing to do is to send one of our Nestor robots—"

"No! Don't be foolish," broke in Susan Calvin.

Schloss said, freezingly, "The Nestors are acquainted with the problems of etherics engineering. They will be ideally—"

"Out of the question. You cannot use one of our positronic robots for such a purpose without my permission. You do not have it and you shall not get it."

"What is the alternative?"

"You must send one of your engineers."

Schloss shook his head violently, "Impossible. The risk involved is too great. If we lose a ship *and* a man—"

"Nevertheless, you may not use a Nestor robot, or any robot."

The general said, "I—I must get in touch with Earth. This whole problem has to go to a higher level."

Susan Calvin said with asperity, "I wouldn't just yet if I were you, general. You will be throwing yourself on the government's mercy without a suggestion or plan of action of your own. You will not come out very well, I am certain."

"But what is there to do?" The general was using his handkerchief again.

"Send a man. There is no alternative."

Schloss had paled to a pasty gray. "It's easy to say, send a man. But whom?"

"I've been considering that problem. Isn't there a young man—his name is Black—whom I met on the occasion of my previous visit to Hyper Base?"

"Dr. Gerald Black?"

"I think so. Yes. He was a bachelor then. Is he still?"

"Yes, I believe so."

"I would suggest then that he be brought here, say, in fifteen minutes, and that meanwhile I have access to his records."

Smoothly she had assumed authority in this situation, and neither Kallner nor Schloss made any attempt to dispute that authority with her.

Black had seen Susan Calvin from a distance on this, her second visit to Hyper Base. He had made no move to cut down the distance. Now that he had been called into her presence, he found himself staring at her with revulsion and distaste. He scarcely noticed Dr. Schloss and General Kallner standing behind her.

He remembered the last time he had faced her thus, undergoing a cold dissection for the sake of a lost robot.

Dr. Calvin's cool gray eyes were fixed steadily on his hot brown ones.

"Dr. Black," she said, "I believe you understand the situation."

Black said, "I do."

"Something will have to be done. The ship is too expensive to lose. The bad publicity will probably mean the end of the project."

Black nodded. "I've been thinking that."

"I hope you've also thought that it will be necessary for

someone to board the *Parsec,* find out what's wrong, and—uh—deactivate it."

There was a moment's pause. Black said harshly, "What fool would go?"

Kallner frowned and looked at Schloss, who bit his lip and looked nowhere.

Susan Calvin said, "There is, of course, the possibility of accidental activation of the hyperfield, in which case the ship may drive beyond all possible reach. On the other hand, it may return somewhere within the solar system. If so, no expense or effort will be spared to recover man and ship."

Black said, "Idiot and ship! Just a correction."

Susan Calvin disregarded the comment. She said, "I have asked General Kallner's permission to put it to you. It is you who must go."

No pause at all here. Black said, in the flattest possible way, "Lady, I'm not volunteering."

"There are not a dozen men on Hyper Base with sufficient knowledge to have any chance at all of carrying this thing through successfully. Of those who have the knowledge, I've selected you on the basis of our previous acquaintanceship. You will bring to this task an understanding—"

"Look, I'm *not* volunteering."

"You have no choice. Surely you will face your responsibility?"

"My responsibility? What makes it mine?"

"The fact that you are best fitted for the job."

"Do you know the risk?"

"I think I do," said Susan Calvin.

"I know you don't. You never saw that chimpanzee. Look, when I said 'idiot and ship' I wasn't expressing an opinion. I was telling you a fact. I'd risk my life if I had to. Not with pleasure, maybe, but I'd risk it. Risking idiocy, a lifetime of animal mindlessness, is something I won't risk, that's all."

Susan Calvin glanced thoughtfully at the young engineer's sweating, angry face.

Black shouted, "Send one of your robots, one of your NS-2 jobs."

The psychologist's eye reflected a kind of cold glitter. She said with deliberation, "Yes, Dr. Schloss suggested that. But the NS-2 robots are leased by our firm, not sold. They cost millions of dollars apiece, you know. I represent the company and I have decided that they are too expensive to be risked in a matter such as this."

Black lifted his hands. They clenched and trembled close to his chest as though he were forcibly restraining them. "You're telling me—you're saying you want me to go instead of a robot because I'm more expendable."

"It comes to that, yes."

"Dr. Calvin," said Black, "I'd see you in hell first."

"That statement might be almost literally true, Dr. Black. As General Kallner will confirm, you are ordered to take this assignment. You are under quasi-military law here, I understand, and if you refuse an assignment, you can be court-martialed. A case like this will mean Mercury prison and I believe that will be close enough to hell to make your statement uncomfortably accurate were I to visit you, though I probably would not. On the other hand, if you agree to board the *Parsec* and carry through this job, it will mean a great deal for your career."

Black glared, red-eyed, at her.

Susan Calvin said, "Give the man five minutes to think about this, General Kallner, and get a ship ready."

Two security guards escorted Black out of the room.

Gerald Black felt cold. His limbs moved as though they were not part of him. It was as though he were watching himself from some remote, safe place, watching himself board a ship and make ready to leave for It and for the *Parsec*.

He couldn't quite believe it. He had bowed his head suddenly and said, "I'll go."

But why?

He had never thought of himself as the hero type. Then why? Partly, of course, there was the threat of Mercury prison. Partly it was the awful reluctance to appear a coward in the eyes of those who knew him, that deeper cowardice that was behind half the bravery in the world.

Mostly, though, it was something else.

Ronson of Interplanetary Press had stopped Black momentarily as he was on his way to the ship. Black looked at Ronson's flushed face and said, "What do you want?"

Ronson babbled, "Listen! When you get back, I want it

exclusive. I'll arrange any payment you want—anything you want—"

Black pushed him aside, sent him sprawling, and walked on.

The ship had a crew of two. Neither spoke to him. Their glances slid over and under and around him. Black didn't mind that. They were scared spitless themselves and their ship was approaching the *Parsec* like a kitten skittering sideways toward the first dog it had ever seen. He could do without *them*.

There was only one face that he kept seeing. The anxious expression of General Kallner and the look of synthetic determination on Schloss's face were momentary punctures on his consciousness. They healed almost at once. It was Susan Calvin's unruffled face that he saw. Her calm expressionlessness as he boarded the ship.

He stared into the blackness where Hyper Base had already disappeared into space—

Susan Calvin! Doctor Susan Calvin! Robopsychologist Susan Calvin! The robot that walks like a woman!

What were her three laws, he wondered. First Law: Thou shalt protect the robot with all thy might and all thy heart and all thy soul. Second Law: Thou shalt hold the interests of U.S. Robots and Mechanical Men, Inc. holy provided it interfereth not with the First Law. Third Law: Thou shalt give passing consideration to a human being provided it interfereth not with the First and Second laws.

Had she ever been young, he wondered savagely? Had she ever felt one honest emotion?

Space! How he wanted to do something—something that would take that frozen look of nothing off her face.

And he would!

By the stars, he would. Let him but get out of this sane and he would see her smashed and her company with her and all the vile brood of robots with them. It was that thought that was driving him more than fear of prison or desire for social prestige. It was that thought that almost robbed him of fear altogether. Almost.

One of the pilots muttered at him, without looking, "You can drop down from here. It's half a mile under."

Black said bitterly, "Aren't you landing?"

"Strict orders not to. The vibration of the landing might—"

"What about the vibration of my landing?"

The pilot said, "I've got my orders."

Black said no more but climbed into his suit and waited for the inner lock to open. A tool kit was welded firmly to the metal of the suit about his right thigh.

Just as he stepped into the lock, the earpieces inside his helmet rumbled at him. "Wish you luck, doctor."

It took a moment for him to realize that it came from the two men aboard ship, pausing in their eagerness to get out of that haunted volume of space to give him that much, anyway.

"Thanks," said Black awkwardly, half resentfully.

And then he was out in space, tumbling slowly as the result of the slightly off-center thrust of feet against outer lock.

He could see the *Parsec* waiting for him, and by looking between his legs at the right moment of the tumble he could see the long hiss of the lateral jets of the ship that had brought him, as it turned to leave.

He was alone! Space, he was alone!

Could any man in history ever have felt so alone?

Would he know, he wondered sickly, if—if anything happened? Would there be any moments of realization? Would he feel his mind fade and the light of reason and thought dim and blank out?

Or would it happen suddenly, like the cut of a force knife?

In either case—

The thought of the chimpanzee, blank-eyed, shivering with mindless terrors, was fresh within him.

The asteroid was twenty feet below him now. It swam through space with an absolutely even motion. Barring human agency, no grain of sand upon it had as much as stirred through astronomical periods of time.

In the ultimate jarlessness of It, some small particle of grit encumbered a delicate working unit on board the *Parsec,* or a speck of impure sludge in the fine oil that bathed some moving part had stopped it.

Perhaps it required only a small vibration, a tiny tremor originating from the collision of mass and mass to unencumber that moving part, bringing it down along its appointed path, creating the hyperfield, blossoming it outward like an incredibly ripening rose.

His body was going to touch It and he drew his limbs together in his anxiety to "hit easy." He did not want to touch the asteroid. His skin crawled with intense aversion.

It came closer.

Now—now—

Nothing!

There was only the continuing touch of the asteroid, the uncanny moments of slowly mounting pressure that resulted from a mass of 250 pounds (himself plus suit) possessing full inertia but no weight to speak of.

Black opened his eyes slowly and let the sight of stars enter. The sun was a glowing marble, its brilliance muted by the polarizing shield over his faceplate. The stars were correspondingly feeble but they made up the familiar arrangement. With sun and constellations normal, he was still in the solar system. He could even see Hyper Base, a small, dim crescent.

He stiffened in shock at the sudden voice in his ear. It was Schloss.

Schloss said, "We've got you in view, Dr. Black. You are not alone!"

Black could have laughed at the phraseology, but he only said in a low, clear voice, "Clear off. If you'll do that, you won't be distracting me."

A pause. Schloss's voice, more cajoling, "If you care to report as you go along, it may relieve the tension."

"You'll get information from me when I get back. Not before." He said it bitterly, and bitterly his metal-encased fingers moved to the control panel in his chest and blanked out the suit's radio. They could talk into a vacuum now. He had his own plans. If he got out of this sane, it would be *his* show.

He got to his feet with infinite caution and stood on It. He swayed a bit as involuntary muscular motions, tricked by the almost total lack of gravity into an endless series of overbalancings, pulled him this way and that. On Hyper Base there was a pseudo-gravitic field to hold them down. Black found that a portion of his mind was sufficiently detached to remember that and appreciate it *in absentia*.

The sun had disappeared behind a crag. The stars wheeled visibly in time to the asteroid's one-hour rotation period.

He could see the *Parsec* from where he stood and now he

moved toward it slowly, carefully—tippy-toe almost. (No vibration. No vibration. The words ran pleadingly through his mind.)

Before he was completely aware of the distance he had crossed, he was at the ship. He was at the foot of the line of hand grips that led to the outer lock.

There he paused.

The ship looked quite normal. Or at least it looked normal except for the circle of steely knobs that girdled it one third of the way up, and a second circle two thirds of the way up. At the moment, they must be straining to become the source poles of the hyperfield.

A strange desire to reach up and fondle one of them came over Black. It was one of those irrational impulses, like the momentary thought, "What if I jumped?" that is almost inevitable when one stares down from a high building.

Black took a deep breath and felt himself go clammy as he spread the fingers of both hands and then lightly, so lightly, put each hand flat against the side of the ship.

Nothing!

He seized the lowest hand grip and pulled himself up, carefully. He longed to be as experienced at null-gravity manipulation as were the construction men. You had to exert enough force to overcome inertia and then stop. Continue the pull a second too long and you would overbalance, career into the side of the ship.

He climbed slowly, tippy-fingers, his legs and hips swaying to the right as his left arm reached upward, to the left as his right arm reached upward.

A dozen rungs, and his fingers hovered over the contact that would open the outer lock. The safety marker was a tiny green smear.

Once again he hesitated. This was the first use he would make of the ship's power. His mind ran over the wiring diagrams and the force distributions. If he pressed the contact, power would be siphoned off the micropile to pull open the massive slab of metal that was the outer lock.

Well?

What was the use? Unless he had some idea as to what was wrong, there was no way of telling the effect of the power diversion. He sighed and touched contact.

Smoothly, with neither jar nor sound, a segment of the ship curled open. Black took one more look at the friendly constellations (they had not changed) and stepped into the softly illuminated cavity. The outer lock closed behind him.

Another contact now. The inner lock had to be opened. Again he paused to consider. Air pressure within the ship would drop ever so slightly as the inner lock opened, and seconds would pass before the ship's electrolyzers could make up the loss.

Well?

The Bosch posterior-plate, to name one item, was sensitive to pressure, but surely not *this* sensitive.

He sighed again, more softly (the skin of his fear was growing calloused) and touched the contact. The inner lock opened.

He stepped into the pilot room of the *Parsec,* and his heart jumped oddly when the first thing he saw was the visiplate, set for reception and powdered with stars. He forced himself to look at them.

Nothing!

Cassiopeia was visible. The constellations were normal and he was inside the *Parsec.* Somehow he could feel the worst was over. Having come so far and remained within the solar system, having kept his mind so far, he felt something that was faintly like confidence begin to seep back.

There was an almost supernatural stillness about the *Parsec.* Black had been in many ships in his life and there had always been the sounds of life, even if only the scuffing of a shoe or a cabin boy humming in the corridor. Here the very beating of his own heart seemed muffled to soundlessness.

The robot in the pilot's seat had its back to him. It indicated by no response that it was aware of his having entered.

Black bared his teeth in a savage grin and said sharply, "Release the bar! Stand up!" The sound of his voice was thunderous in the close quarters.

Too late he dreaded the air vibrations his voice set up, but the stars on the visiplate remained unchanged.

The robot, of course, did not stir. It could receive no sensations of any sort. It could not even respond to the First Law. It was frozen in the unending middle of what should have been almost instantaneous process.

He remembered the orders it had been given. They were open to no misunderstanding: "Seize the bar with a firm grip. Pull it toward you firmly. Firmly! Maintain your hold until the control board informs you that you have passed through hyperspace twice."

Well, it had not yet passed through hyperspace once.

Carefully, he moved closer to the robot. It sat there with the bar pulled firmly back between its knees. That brought the trigger mechanism almost into place. The temperature of his metal hands then curled that trigger, thermocouple fashion, just sufficiently for contact to be made. Automatically Black glanced at the thermometer reading set into the control board. The robot's hands were at 37 Centigrade, as they should be.

He thought sardonically, Fine thing. I'm alone with this machine and I can't do anything about it.

What he would have liked to do was take a crowbar to it and smash it to filings. He enjoyed the flavor of that thought. He could see the horror on Susan Calvin's face (if any horror could creep through the ice, the horror of a smashed robot was it). Like all positronic robots, this one-shot was owned by U.S. Robots, had been made there, had been tested there.

And having extracted what juice he could out of imaginary revenge, he sobered and looked about the ship.

After all, progress so far had been zero.

Slowly, he removed his suit. Gently, he laid it on the rack. Gingerly, he walked from room to room, studying the large interlocking surfaces of the hyperatomic motor, following the cables, inspecting the field relays.

He touched nothing. There were a dozen ways of deactivating the hyperfield, but each one would be ruinous unless he knew at least approximately where the error lay and let his exact course of procedure be guided by that.

He found himself back at the control panel and cried in exasperation at the grave stolidity of the robot's broad back, "Tell me, will you? What's wrong?"

There was the urge to attack the ship's machinery at random. Tear at it and get it over with. He repressed the impulse firmly. If it took him a week, he would deduce, somehow, the proper point of attack. He owed that much to Dr. Susan Calvin and his plans for her.

He turned slowly on his heel and considered. Every part of

the ship, from the engine itself to each individual two-way toggle switch, had been exhaustively checked and tested on Hyper Base. It was almost impossible to believe that anything could go wrong. There wasn't a thing on board ship—

Well, yes, there was, of course. The robot! That had been tested at U.S. Robots and they, blast their devil's hides, could be assumed to be competent.

What was it everyone always said: A robot can just naturally do a better job.

It was the normal assumption, based in part on U.S. Robots' own advertising campaigns. They could make a robot that would be better than a man for a given purpose. Not "as good as a man," but "better than a man."

And as Gerald Black stared at the robot and thought that, his brows contracted under his low forehead and his look became compounded of astonishment and a wild hope.

He approached and circled the robot. He stared at its arms holding the control bar in trigger position, holding it forever so, unless the ship jumped or the robot's own power supply gave out.

Black breathed, "I bet. I *bet*."

He stepped away, considered deeply. He said, "It's *got* to be."

He turned on ship's radio. Its carrier beam was already focused on Hyper Base. He barked into the mouthpiece, "Hey, Schloss."

Schloss was prompt in his answer. "Great Space, Black—"

"Never mind," said Black crisply. "No speeches. I just want to make sure you're watching."

"Yes, of course. We all are. Look—"

But Black turned off the radio. He grinned with tight one-sidedness at the TV camera inside the pilot room and chose a portion of the hyperfield mechanism that would be in view. He didn't know how many people would be in the viewing room. There might be only Kallner, Schloss and Susan Calvin. There might be all personnel. In any case, he would give them something to watch.

Relay Box #3 was adequate for the purpose, he decided. It was located in a wall recess, coated over with a smooth cold-seamed panel. Black reached into his tool kit and removed the splayed, blunt-edged seamer. He pushed his space suit further back on the rack (having turned it to bring the tool kit in reach) and turned to the relay box.

Ignoring a last tingle of uneasiness, Black brought up the seamer, made contact at three separated points along the cold seam. The tool's force field worked deftly and quickly, the handle growing a trifle warm in his hand as the surge of energy came and left. The panel swung free.

He glanced quickly, almost involuntarily, at the ship's vis-iplate. The stars were normal. He, himself, felt normal.

That was the last bit of encouragement he needed. He raised his foot and smashed his shoe down on the feather-delicate mechanism within the recess.

There was a splinter of glass, a twisting of metal, and a tiny spray of mercury droplets—

Black breathed heavily. He turned on the radio once more. "Still there, Schloss?"

"Yes, but—"

"Then I report the hyperfield on board the *Parsec* to be deactivated. Come and get me."

Gerald Black felt no more the hero than when he had left for the *Parsec,* but he found himself one just the same. The men who had brought him to the small asteroid came to take him off. They landed this time. They clapped his back.

Hyper Base was a crowded mass of waiting personnel when the ship arrived, and Black was cheered. He waved at the throng and grinned, as was a hero's obligation, but he felt no triumph inside. Not yet. Only anticipation. Triumph would come later, when he met Susan Calvin.

He paused before descending from the ship. He looked for her and did not see her. General Kallner was there, waiting, with all his soldierly stiffness restored and a bluff look of approval firmly plastered on his face. Mayer Schloss smiled nervously at him. Ronson of Interplanetary Press waved frantically. Susan Calvin was nowhere.

He brushed Kallner and Schloss aside when he landed. "I'm going to wash and eat first."

He had no doubts but that, for the moment at least, he could dictate terms to the general or to anybody.

The security guards made a way for him. He bathed and ate leisurely in enforced isolation, he himself being solely responsible for the enforcement. Then he called Ronson of Interplanetary and talked to him briefly. He waited for the return call before he felt he could relax thoroughly. It had all worked out so much better than he had expected. The very failure of the ship had conspired perfectly with him.

Finally he called the general's office and ordered a conference. It was what it amounted to—orders. Major General Kallner all but said, "Yes, sir."

They were together again. Gerald Black, Kallner, Schloss—even Susan Calvin. But it was Black who was dominant now. The robopsychologist, graven-faced as ever, as unimpressed by triumph as by disaster, had nevertheless seemed by some subtle change of attitude to have relinquished the spotlight.

Dr. Schloss nibbled a thumbnail and began by saying, cautiously, "Dr. Black, we are all very grateful for your bravery and success." Then, as though to institute a healthy deflation at once, he added, "Still, smashing the relay box with your heel was imprudent and—well, it was an action that scarcely deserved success."

Black said, "It was an action that could scarcely have avoided success. You see," (this was bomb number one) "by that time I knew what had gone wrong."

Schloss rose to his feet. "You did? Are you sure?"

"Go there yourself. It's safe now. I'll tell you what to look for."

Schloss sat down again, slowly. General Kallner was enthusiastic. "Why, this is the best yet, if true."

"It's true," said Black. His eyes slid to Susan Calvin, who said nothing.

Black was enjoying the sensation of power. He released bomb number two by saying: "It was the robot, of course. Did you hear that, Dr. Calvin?"

Susan Calvin spoke for the first time. "I hear it. I rather expected it, as a matter of fact. It was the only piece of equipment on board ship that had not been tested at Hyper Base."

For a moment Black felt dashed. He said, "You said nothing of that."

Dr. Calvin said, "As Dr. Schloss said several times, I am not an etherics expert. My guess, and it was no more than that, might easily have been wrong. I felt I had no right to prejudice you in advance of your mission."

Black said, "All right, did you happen to guess *how* it went wrong?"

"No sir."

"Why, it was made better than a man. That's what the trouble was. Isn't it strange that the trouble should rest with the very specialty of U.S. Robots? They make robots better than men, I understand."

He was slashing at her with words now but she did not rise to his bait.

Instead, she sighed. "My dear Dr. Black. I am not responsible for the slogans of our sales-promotion department."

Black felt dashed again. She wasn't an easy woman to handle, this Calvin. He said, "Your people built a robot to replace a man at the controls of the *Parsec*. He had to pull the control bar toward himself, place it in position and let the heat of his hands twist the trigger to make final contact. Simple enough, Dr. Calvin?"

"Simple enough, Dr. Black."

"And if the robot had been made no better than a man, he would have succeeded. Unfortunately, U.S. Robots felt compelled to make it better than a man. The robot was told to pull back the control bar firmly. The word was repeated, strengthened, emphasized. So the robot did what it was told. It pulled it back firmly. There was only one trouble. He was easily ten times stronger than the ordinary human being for whom the control bar was designed."

"Are you implying—"

"I'm *saying* the bar bent. It bent back just enough to misplace the trigger. When the heat of the robot's hand twisted the thermocouple, it did *not* make contact." He grinned. "This isn't the failure of just one robot, Dr. Calvin. It's symbolic of the failure of the robot idea."

"Come now, Dr. Black," said Susan Calvin icily, "you're drowning logic in missionary psychology. The robot was equipped with adequate understanding as well as with brute force. Had the men who gave it its orders used quantitative terms rather than the foolish adverb 'firmly,' this would not have happened. Had they said, 'apply a pull of fifty-five pounds,' all would have been well."

"What you are saying," said Black, "is that the inadequacy of a robot must be made up for by the ingenuity and intelligence of a man. I assure you that the people back on Earth will look at it in that way and will not be in the mood to excuse U.S. Robots for the fiasco."

Major General Kallner said quickly, with a return of authority to his voice, "Now wait, Black, all that has happened is obviously classified information."

"In fact," said Schloss suddenly, "your theory hasn't been checked yet. We'll send a party to the ship and find out. It may not be the robot at all."

"You'll take care to make that discovery, will you? I wonder if the people will believe an interested party. Besides which, I have one more thing to tell you." He readied bomb number three and said, "As of this moment, I'm resigning from this man's project. I'm quitting."

"Why?" asked Susan Calvin.

"Because, as you said, Dr. Calvin, I am a missionary," said Black, smiling. "I have a mission. I feel I owe it to the people of Earth to tell them that the age of the robots has reached the point where human life is valued less than robot life. It is now possible to order a man into danger because a robot is too precious to risk. I believe Earthmen should hear that. Many men have many reservations about robots as is. U.S. Robots has not yet succeeded in making it legally permissible to use robots on the planet Earth itself. I believe what I have to say, Dr. Calvin, will complete the matter. For this day's work, Dr. Calvin, you and your company and your robots will be wiped off the face of the solar system."

He was forewarning her, Black knew; he was forearming her, but he could not forego this scene. He had lived for this very moment ever since he had first left for the *Parsec,* and he could not give it up.

He all but gloated at the momentary glitter in Susan Calvin's pale eyes and at the faintest flush in her cheeks. He thought, How do you feel now, madam scientist?

Kallner said, "You will not be permitted to resign, Black, nor will you be permitted—"

"How can you stop me, general? I'm a hero, haven't you heard? And old Mother Earth *will* make much of its heroes. It always has. They'll want to hear from me and they'll believe anything I say. And they won't like it if I'm interfered with, at least not while I'm a fresh, brand-new hero. I've already talked to Ronson of Interplanetary Press and told him I had something big for them, something that would rock every government official and science director right out of the chair plush, so Interplanetary will be first in line, waiting to hear from me. So what can you do except to have me shot? And I think you'd be worse off after that if you tried it."

Black's revenge was complete. He had spared no word. He had hampered himself not in the least. He rose to go.

"One moment, Dr. Black," said Susan Calvin. Her low voice carried authority.

Black turned involuntarily, like a schoolboy at his teacher's voice, but he counteracted that gesture by a deliberately mocking, "You have an explanation to make, I suppose?"

"Not at all," she said primly. "You have explained for me, and quite well. I chose you because I knew you would understand, though I thought you would understand sooner. I had had contact with you before. I knew you disliked robots and would, therefore, be under no illusions concerning them. From your records, which I asked to see before you were given your assignment, I saw that you had expressed disapproval of this robot-through-hyperspace experiment. Your superiors held that against you, but I thought it a point in your favor."

"What are you talking about, doctor, if you'll excuse my rudeness?"

"The fact that you should have understood why no robot could have been sent on this mission. What was it you yourself said? Something about a robot's inadequacies having to be balanced by the ingenuity and intelligence of a man. Exactly so, young man, exactly so. Robots have no ingenuity. Their minds are finite and can be calculated to the last decimal. That, in fact, is my job.

"Now if a robot is given an order, a *precise* order, he can follow it. If the order is not precise, he cannot correct his own mistake without further orders. Isn't that what you reported concerning the robot on the ship? How then can we send a robot to find a flaw in a mechanism when we cannot possibly give precise orders, since we know nothing about the flaw ourselves? 'Find out what's wrong' is not an order you can give to a robot; only to a man. The human brain, so far at least, is beyond calculation."

Black sat down abruptly and stared at the psychologist in

dismay. Her words struck sharply on a substratum of under-standing that had been larded over with emotion. He found himself unable to refute her. Worse than that, a feeling of defeat encompassed him.

He said, "You might have said this before I left."

"I might have," agreed Dr. Calvin, "but I noticed your very natural fear for your sanity. Such an overwhelming concern would easily have hampered your efficiency as an investigator, and it occurred to me to let you think that my only motive in sending you was that I valued a robot more. That, I thought, would make you angry, and anger, my dear Dr. Black, is some-times a very useful emotion. At least, an angry man is never quite as afraid as he would be otherwise. It worked out nicely, I think." She folded her hands loosely in her lap and came as near a smile as she ever had in her life.

Black said, "I'll be damned."

Susan Calvin said, "So now, if you'll take my advice, return to your job, accept your status as hero, and tell your reporter friend the details of your brave deed. Let that be the big news you promised him."

Slowly, reluctantly, Black nodded.

Schloss looked relieved; Kallner burst into a toothy smile. They held out hands, not having said a word in all the time that Susan Calvin had spoken, and not saying a word now.

Black took their hands and shook them with some reserve. He said, "It's your part that should be publicized, Dr. Calvin."

Susan Calvin said icily, "Don't be a fool, young man. This is my job."

Lenny

"Lenny" (which appeared in the January 1958 issue of Infinity Science Fiction) was written under unusual circumstances. I am, now and then, overawed into going on vacation against my peevishly expressed desires not to. My wife, who can be quite overawing considering she is such a sweet, soft-voiced thing, is quite insensitive to my explanations that vacations are very hard on my nervous system because I am restless in the absence of a typewriter.

She said calmly, "Take a typewriter with you."

So I did, and for a couple of hours each morning I took it out on the lawn of the resort hotel (my wife sweetly and soft-voicedly insisting in the sovereign virtues of sun and fresh air—ugh!), placed it on a rickety table, weighted down various sheets of paper with stones and got to work.

Not a morning passed without interruptions by someone wanting to know what I was doing. I explained and when they finally understood that I was working, they regarded me with no attempt at concealing their hostility.

The word went round that I was a dangerous radical attempting to undermine the Great American Vacation.

I managed, somehow, to finish, and my lovable attic room never looked more lovable than it did when I returned. It took me some time to get back to work. First I had to kiss all the walls.

Lenny

United States Robots and Mechanical Men, Inc., had a problem. The problem was people.

Peter Bogert, Senior Mathematician, was on his way to Assembly when he encountered Alfred Lanning, Research Director. Lanning was bending his ferocious white eyebrows together and staring down across the railing into the computer room.

On the floor below the balcony, a trickle of humanity of both sexes and various ages was looking about curiously, while a guide intoned a set speech about robotic computing.

"This computer you see before you," he said, "is the largest of its type in the world. It contains five million three hundred thousand cryotrons and is capable of dealing simultaneously with over one hundred thousand variables. With its help, U.S. Robots is able to design with precision the positronic brains of new models.

"The requirements are fed in on tape which is perforated by the action of this keyboard—something like a very complicated typewriter or linotype machine, except that it does not deal with letters but with concepts. Statements are broken down into the symbolic logic equivalents and those in turn converted to perforation patterns.

"The computer can, in less than one hour, present our scientists with a design for a brain which will give all the necessary positronic paths to make a robot . . ."

Alfred Lanning looked up at last and noticed the other. "Ah, Peter," he said.

Bogert raised both hands to smooth down his already perfectly smooth and glossy head of black hair. He said, "You don't look as though you think much of this, Alfred."

Lanning grunted. The idea of public guided tours of U.S. Robots was a fairly recent origin, and was supposed to serve a dual function. On the one hand, the theory went, it allowed people to see robots at close quarters and counter their almost instinctive fear of the mechanical objects through increased familiarity. And on the other hand, it was supposed to interest at least an occasional person in taking up robotics research as a life work.

"You know I don't," Lanning said finally. "Once a week, work is disrupted. Considering the man-hours lost, the return is insufficient."

"Still no rise in job applications, then?"

"Oh, some, but only in the categories where the need isn't vital. It's research men that are needed. You know that. The trouble is that with robots forbidden on Earth itself, there's something unpopular about being a roboticist."

"The damned Frankenstein complex," said Bogert, consciously imitating one of the other's pet phrases.

Lanning missed the gentle jab. He said, "I ought to be used to it, but I never will. You'd think that by now every human being on Earth would know that the Three Laws represented a perfect safeguard; that robots are simply not dangerous. Take this bunch." He glowered down. "Look at them. Most of them go through the robot assembly room for the thrill of fear, like riding a roller coaster. Then when they enter the room with the MEC model—damn it, Peter, a MEC model that will do nothing on God's green Earth but take two steps forward, say 'Pleased to meet you, sir,' shake hands, then take two steps back—they back away and mothers snatch up their kids. How do we expect to get brainwork out of such idiots?"

Bogert had no answer. Together, they stared down once again at the line of sightseers, now passing out of the computer room and into the positronic brain assembly section. Then they left. They did not, as it turned out, observe Mortimer W. Jacobson, age 16—who, to do him complete justice, meant no harm whatever.

In fact, it could not even be said to be Mortimer's fault. The day of the week on which the tour took place was known to all workers. All devices in its path ought to have been carefully neutralized or locked, since it was unreasonable to expect human beings to withstand the temptation to handle knobs, keys, handles and pushbuttons. In addition, the guide ought to have been very carefully on the watch for those who succumbed.

But, at the time, the guide had passed into the next room and Mortimer was tailing the line. He passed the keyboard on which instructions were fed into the computer. He had no way of suspecting that the plans for a new robot design were being fed into it at that moment, or, being a good kid, he would have avoided the keyboard. He had no way of knowing that, by what amounted to almost criminal negligence, a technician had not inactivated the keyboard.

So Mortimer touched the keys at random as though he were playing a musical instrument.

He did not notice that a section of perforated tape stretched itself out of the instrument in another part of the room—soundlessly, unobtrusively.

Nor did the technician, when he returned, discover any sign of tampering. He felt a little uneasy at noticing that the keyboard was live, but did not think to check. After a few minutes, even his first trifling uneasiness was gone, and he continued feeding data into the computer.

As for Mortimer, neither then, nor ever afterward, did he know what he had done.

The new LNE model was designed for the mining of boron in the asteroid belt. The boron hydrides were increasing in value yearly as primers for the proton micropiles that carried the ultimate load of power production on spaceships, and Earth's own meager supply was running thin.

Physically, that meant that the LNE robots would have to

be equipped with eyes sensitive to those lines prominent in the spectroscopic analysis of boron ores and the type of limbs most useful for the working up of ore to finished product. As always, though, the mental equipment was the major problem.

The first LNE positronic brain had been completed now. It was the prototype and would join all other prototypes in U.S. Robots' collection. When finally tested, others would then be manufactured for leasing (never selling) to mining corporations.

LNE-Prototype was complete now. Tall, straight, polished, it looked from outside like any of a number of not-too-specialized robot models.

The technician in charge, guided by the directions for testing in the *Handbook of Robotics*, said, "How are you?"

The indicated answer was to have been, "I am well and ready to begin my functions. I trust you are well, too," or some trivial modification thereof.

This first exchange served no purpose but to show that the robot could hear, understand a routine question, and make a routine reply congruent with what one would expect of a robotic attitude. Beginning from there, one could pass on to more complicated matters that would test the different Laws and their interaction with the specialized knowledge of each particular model.

So the technician said, "How are you?" He was instantly jolted by the nature of LNE-Prototype's voice. It had a quality like no robotic voice he had ever heard (and he had heard many). It formed syllables like the chimes of a low-pitched celeste.

So surprising was this that it was only after several moments that the technician heard, in retrospect, the syllables that had been formed by those heavenly tones.

They were, "Da, da, da, goo."

The robot still stood tall and straight but its right hand crept upward and a finger went into its mouth.

The technician stared in absolute horror and bolted. He locked the door behind him and, from another room, put in an emergency call to Dr. Susan Calvin.

Dr. Susan Calvin was U.S. Robots' (and, virtually, mankind's) only robopsychologist. She did not have to go very far in her testing of LNE-Prototype before she called very peremptorily for a transcript of the computer-drawn plans of the positronic brain-paths and the taped instructions that had directed them. After some study, she, in turn, sent for Bogert.

Her iron-gray hair was drawn severely back; her cold face, with its strong vertical lines marked off by the horizontal gash of the pale, thin-lipped mouth, turned intensely upon him.

"What *is* this, Peter?"

Bogert studied the passages she pointed out with increasing stupefaction and said, "Good Lord, Susan, it makes no sense."

"It most certainly doesn't. How did it get into the instructions?"

The technician in charge, called upon, swore in all sincerity that it was none of his doing, and that he could not account for it. The computer checked out negative for all attempts at flaw-finding.

"The positronic brain," said Susan Calvin, thoughtfully, "is past redemption. So many of the higher functions have been cancelled out by these meaningless directions that the result is very like a human baby."

Bogert looked surprised, and Susan Calvin took on a frozen attitude at once, as she always did at the least expressed or implied doubt of her word. She said, "We make every effort to make a robot as mentally like a man as possible. Eliminate what we call the adult functions and what is naturally left is a human infant, mentally speaking. Why do you look so surprised, Peter?"

LNE-Prototype, who showed no signs of understanding any of the things that were going on around it, suddenly slipped into a sitting position and began a minute examination of its feet.

Bogert stared at it. "It's a shame to have to dismantle the creature. It's a handsome job."

"Dismantle it?" said the robopsychologist forcefully.

"Of course, Susan. What's the use of this thing? Good Lord, if there's one object completely and abysmally useless it's a robot without a job it can perform. You don't pretend there's a job this thing can do, do you?"

"No, of course not."

"Well, then?"

Susan Calvin said, stubbornly, "I want to conduct more tests."

Bogert looked at her with a moment's impatience, then shrugged. If there was one person at U.S. Robots with whom it was useless to dispute, surely that was Susan Calvin. Robots were all she loved, and long association with them, it seemed to Bogert, had deprived her of any appearance of humanity. She was no more to be argued out of a decision than was a triggered micropile to be argued out of operating.

"What's the use?" he breathed; then aloud, hastily: "Will you let us know when your tests are complete?"

"I will," she said. "Come, Lenny."

(LNE, thought Bogert. That becomes Lenny. Inevitable.)

Susan Calvin held out her hand but the robot only stared at it. Gently, the robopsychologist reached for the robot's hand and took it. Lenny rose smoothly to its feet (its mechanical coordination, at least, worked well). Together they walked out, robot topping woman by two feet. Many eyes followed them curiously down the long corridors.

One wall of Susan Calvin's laboratory, the one opening directly off her private office, was covered with a highly magnified reproduction of a positronic-path chart. Susan Calvin had studied it with absorption for the better part of a month.

She was considering it now, carefully, tracing the blunted paths through their contortions. Behind her, Lenny sat on the floor, moving its legs apart and together, crooning meaningless syllables to itself in a voice so beautiful that one could listen to the nonsense and be ravished.

Susan Calvin turned to the robot, "Lenny—Lenny—"

She repeated this patiently until finally Lenny looked up and made an inquiring sound. The robopsychologist allowed a glimmer of pleasure to cross her face fleetingly. The robot's attention was being gained in progressively shorter intervals.

She said, "Raise your hand, Lenny. Hand—up. Hand—up."

Lenny followed the movement with its eyes. Up, down, up, down. Then it made an abortive gesture with its own hand and chimed, "Eh—uh."

"Very good, Lenny," said Susan Calvin, gravely. "Try it again. Hand—up."

Very gently, she reached out her own hand, took the robot's, and raised it, lowered it. "Hand—up. Hand—up."

A voice from her office called and interrupted. "Susan?"

Calvin halted with a tightening of her lips. "What is it, Alfred?"

The research director walked in, and looked at the chart on the wall and at the robot. "Still at it?"

"I'm at my work, yes."

"Well, you know, Susan . . ." He took out a cigar, staring at it hard, and made as though to bite off the end. In doing so, his eyes met the woman's stern look of disapproval; and he put the cigar away and began over. "Well, you know, Susan, the LNE model is in production now."

"So I've heard. Is there something in connection with it you wish of me?"

"No-o. Still, the mere fact that it is in production and is doing well means that working with this messed-up specimen is useless. Shouldn't it be scrapped?"

"In short, Alfred, you are annoyed that I am wasting my so-valuable time. Feel relieved. My time is not being wasted. I am *working* with this robot."

"But the work has no meaning."

"I'll be the judge of that, Alfred." Her voice was ominously quiet, and Lanning thought it wiser to shift his ground.

"Will you tell me what meaning it has? What are you doing with it right now, for instance?"

"I'm trying to get it to raise its hand on the word of command. I'm trying to get it to imitate the sound of the word."

As though on cue, Lenny said, "Eh—uh" and raised its hand waveringly.

Lanning shook his head. "That voice is amazing. How does it happen?"

Susan Calvin said, "I don't quite know. Its transmitter is a normal one. It could speak normally, I'm sure. It doesn't, however; it speaks like this as a consequence of something in the positronic paths that I have not yet pinpointed."

"Well, pinpoint it, for Heaven's sake. Speech like that might be useful."

"Oh, then there is some possible use in my studies on Lenny?"

Lanning shrugged in embarrassment. "Oh, well, it's a minor point."

"I'm sorry you don't see the major points, then," said Susan Calvin with asperity, "which are much more important, but that's not my fault. Would you leave now, Alfred, and let me go on with my work?"

Lanning got to his cigar, eventually, in Bogert's office. He said, sourly, "That woman is growing more peculiar daily."

Bogert understood perfectly. In the U.S. Robots and Mechanical Men Corporation, there was only one that woman. He said, "Is she still scuffing about with that pseudo-robot—that Lenny of hers?"

"Trying to get it to talk, so help me."

Bogert shrugged. "Points up the company problem. I mean, about getting qualified personnel for research. If we had other robopsychologists, we could retire Susan. Incidentally, I presume the directors' meeting scheduled for tomorrow is for the purpose of dealing with the procurement problem?"

Lanning nodded and looked at his cigar as though it didn't taste good. "Yes. Quality, though, not quantity. We've raised wages until there's a steady stream of applicants—those who are interested primarily in money. The trick is to get those who are interested primarily in robotics—a few more like Susan Calvin."

"Hell, no. Not like her."

"Well, not like her personally. But you'll have to admit, Peter, that she's single-minded about robots. She has no other interest in life."

"I know. And that's exactly what makes her so unbearable."

Lanning nodded. He had lost count of the many times it would have done his soul good to have fired Susan Calvin. He had also lost count of the number of millions of dollars she had at one time or another saved the company. She was a truly indispensable woman and would remain one until she died—or until they could lick the problem of finding men and women of her own high caliber who were interested in robotic research.

He said, "I think we'll cut down on the tour business."

Peter shrugged. "If you say so. But meanwhile, seriously, what do we do about Susan? She can easily tie herself up with Lenny indefinitely. You know how she is when she gets what she considers an interesting problem."

"What *can* we do?" said Lanning. "If we become too anxious to pull her off, she'll stay on out of feminine contrariness. In the last analysis, we can't force her to do anything."

The dark-haired mathematician smiled. "I wouldn't ever apply the adjective 'feminine' to any part of her."

"Oh, well," said Lanning, grumpily. "At least, it won't do anyone any actual harm."

In that, if in nothing else, he was wrong.

The emergency signal is always a tension-making thing in any large industrial establishment. Such signals had sounded in the history of U.S. Robots a dozen times—for fire, flood, riot and insurrection.

But one thing had never occurred in all that time. Never had the particular signal indicating "Robot out of control" sounded. No one ever expected it to sound. It was only installed at government insistence. ("Damn the Frankenstein complex," Lanning would mutter on those rare occasions when he thought of it.)

Now, finally, the shrill siren rose and fell at ten-second intervals, and practically no worker from the President of the Board of Directors down to the newest janitor's assistant recognized the significance of the strange sound for a few moments. After those moments passed, there was a massive convergence of armed guards and medical men to the indicated area of danger and U.S. Robots was struck with paralysis.

Charles Randow, computing technician, was taken off to hospital level with a broken arm. There was no other damage. No other physical damage.

"But the moral damage," roared Lanning, "is beyond estimation."

Susan Calvin faced him, murderously calm. "You will do nothing to Lenny. Nothing. Do you understand?"

"Do *you* understand, Susan? That thing has hurt a human being. It has broken First Law. Don't you know what First Law is?"

"You will do nothing to Lenny."

"For God's sake, Susan, do I have to tell *you* First Law? *A robot may not harm a human being or, through inaction, allow a human being to come to harm.* Our entire position depends on the fact that First Law is rigidly observed by all robots of all types. If the public should hear, and they will hear, that there was an exception, even one exception, we might be forced to close down altogether. Our only chance of survival would be to announce at once that the robot involved had been destroyed, explain the circumstances, and hope that the public can be convinced that it will never happen again."

"I would like to find out exactly what happened," said Susan Calvin. "I was not present at the time and I would like to know exactly what the Randow boy was doing in my laboratories without my permission."

"The important thing that happened," said Lanning, "is obvious. Your robot struck Randow and the damn fool flashed the 'Robot out of control' button and made a case of it. But your robot struck him and inflicted damage to the extent of a broken arm. The truth is your Lenny is so distorted it lacks First Law and it must be destroyed."

"It does *not* lack First Law. I have studied its brain-paths and know it does not lack it."

"Then how could it strike a man?" Desperation turned him to sarcasm. "Ask Lenny. Surely you have taught it to speak by now."

Susan Calvin's cheeks flushed a painful pink. She said, "I prefer to interview the victim. And in my absence, Alfred, I want my offices sealed tight, with Lenny inside. I want no one to approach him. If any harm comes to him while I am gone, this company will not see me again under any circumstances."

"Will you agree to its destruction, if it has broken First Law?"

"Yes," said Susan Calvin, "because I know it hasn't."

Charles Randow lay in bed with his arm set and in a cast. His major suffering was still from the shock of those few moments in which he thought a robot was advancing on him with murder in its positronic mind. No other human had ever had such reason to fear direct robotic harm as he had just then. He had had a unique experience.

Susan Calvin and Alfred Lanning stood beside his bed now; Peter Bogert, who had met them on the way, was with them. Doctors and nurses had been shooed out.

Susan Calvin said, "Now—what happened?"

Randow was daunted. He muttered, "The thing hit me in the arm. It was coming at me."

Calvin said, "Move further back in the story. What were you doing in my laboratory without authorization?"

The young computer swallowed, and the Adam's apple in his thin neck bobbed noticeably. He was high-cheekboned and abnormally pale. He said, "We all knew about your robot. The word is you were trying to teach it to talk like a musical instrument. There were bets going as to whether it talked or not. Some said—uh—you could teach a gatepost to talk."

"I suppose," said Susan Calvin, freezingly, "that is meant as a compliment. What did that have to do with you?"

"I was supposed to go in there and settle matters—see if it would talk, you know. We swiped a key to your place and I waited till you were gone and went in. We had a lottery on who was to do it. I lost."

"Then?"

"I tried to get it to talk and it hit me."

"What do you mean, you tried to get it to talk? How did you try?"

"I—I asked it questions, but it wouldn't say anything, and I had to give the thing a fair shake, so I kind of—yelled at it, and—"

"And?"

There was a long pause. Under Susan Calvin's unwavering stare, Randow finally said, "I tried to scare it into saying something." He added defensively, "I had to give the thing a fair shake."

"How did you try to scare it?"

"I pretended to take a punch at it."

"And it brushed your arm aside?"

"It *hit* my arm."

"Very well. That's all." To Lanning and Bogert, she said, "Come, gentlemen."

At the doorway, she turned back to Randow. "I can settle the bets going around, if you are still interested. Lenny can speak a few words quite well."

They said nothing until they were in Susan Calvin's office. Its walls were lined with her books, some of which she had written herself. It retained the patina of her own frigid, carefully ordered personality. It had only one chair in it and she sat down. Lanning and Bogert remained standing.

She said, "Lenny only defended itself. That is the Third Law: *A robot must protect its own existence.*"

"Except," said Lanning forcefully, *"when this conflicts with the First or Second Laws.* Complete the statement! Lenny had no right to defend itself in any way at the cost of harm, however minor, to a human being."

"Nor did it," shot back Calvin, *"knowingly.* Lenny has an aborted brain. It had no way of knowing its own strength or the weakness of humans. In brushing aside the threatening arm of a human being it could not know the bone would break. In human terms, no moral blame can be attached to an individual who honestly cannot differentiate good and evil."

Bogert interrupted, soothingly, "Now, Susan, *we* don't blame. *We* understand that Lenny is the equivalent of a baby, humanly speaking, and we don't blame it. But the public will. U.S. Robots will be closed down."

"Quite the opposite. If you had the brains of a flea, Peter, you would see that this is the opportunity U.S. Robots is waiting for. That this will solve its problems."

Lanning hunched his white eyebrows low. He said, softly, "What problems, Susan?"

"Isn't the corporation concerned about maintaining our research personnel at the present—Heaven help us—high level?"

"We certainly are."

"Well, what are you offering prospective researchers? Excitement? Novelty? The thrill of piercing the unknown? No! You offer them salaries and the assurance of no problems."

Bogert said, "How do you mean, no problems?"

"Are there problems?" shot back Susan Calvin. "What kind of robots do we turn out? Fully developed robots, fit for their tasks. An industry tells us what it needs; a computer designs the brain; machinery forms the robot; and there it is, complete and done. Peter, some time ago, you asked me with reference to Lenny what its use was. What's the use, you said, of a robot that was not designed for any job? Now I ask you—what's the use of a robot designed for only one job? It begins and ends in the same place. The LNE models mine boron. If beryllium is needed, they are useless. If boron technology enters a new phase, they become useless. A human being so designed would be sub-human. A robot so designed is sub-robotic."

"Do you want a versatile robot?" asked Lanning, incredulously.

"Why not?" demanded the robopsychologist. "Why not? I've been handed a robot with a brain almost completely stultified. I've been teaching it, and you, Alfred, asked me what was the use of that. Perhaps very little as far as Lenny itself is concerned, since it will never progress beyond the five-year-old level on a human scale. But what's the use in general? A very great deal, if you consider it as a study in the abstract problem of *learning how to teach robots*. I have learned ways to short-circuit neighboring pathways in order to create new ones. More study will yield better, more subtle and more efficient techniques of doing so."

"Well?"

"Suppose you started with a positronic brain that had all the basic pathways carefully outlined but none of the secondaries. Suppose you then started creating secondaries. You could sell basic robots designed for instruction; robots that could be modelled to a job, and then modelled to another, if necessary. Robots would become as versatile as human beings. *Robots could learn!*"

They stared at her.

She said, impatiently, "You still don't understand, do you?"

"I understand what you are saying," said Lanning.

"Don't you understand that with a completely new field of research and completely new techniques to be developed, with a completely new area of the unknown to be penetrated, youngsters will feel a new urge to enter robotics? Try it and see."

"May I point out," said Bogert, smoothly, "that this is dangerous. Beginning with ignorant robots such as Lenny will mean that one could never trust First Law—exactly as turned out in Lenny's case."

"Exactly. Advertise the fact."

"*Advertise it!*"

"Of course. Broadcast the danger. Explain that you will set up a new research institute on the moon, if Earth's population chooses not to allow this sort of thing to go on upon Earth, but stress the danger to the possible applicants by all means."

Lanning said, "For God's sake, why?"

"Because the spice of danger will add to the lure. Do you think nuclear technology involves no danger and spationautics no peril? Has your lure of absolute security been doing the trick for you? Has it helped you to cater to the Frankenstein complex you all despise so? Try something else then, something that has worked in other fields."

There was a sound from beyond the door that led to Calvin's

personal laboratories. It was the chiming sound of Lenny.

The robopsychologist broke off instantly, listening. She said, "Excuse me. I think Lenny is calling me."

"Can it call you?" said Lanning.

"I said I've managed to teach it a few words." She stepped toward the door, a little flustered. "If you will wait for me—"

They watched her leave and were silent for a moment. Then Lanning said, "Do you think there's anything to what she says, Peter?"

"Just possibly, Alfred," said Bogert. "Just possibly. Enough for us to bring the matter up at the directors' meeting and see what they say. After all, the fat *is* in the fire. A robot has harmed a human being and knowledge of it is public. As Susan says, we might as well try to turn the matter to our advantage. Of course, I distrust her motives in all this."

"How do you mean?"

"Even if all she has said is perfectly true, it is only rationalization as far as she is concerned. Her motive in all this is her desire to hold on to this robot. If we pressed her," (and the mathematician smiled at the incongruous literal meaning of the phrase) "she would say it was to continue learning techniques of teaching robots, but I think she has found another use for Lenny. A rather unique one that would fit only Susan of all women."

"I don't get your drift."

Bogert said, "Did you hear what the robot was calling?"

"Well, no, I didn't quite—" began Lanning, when the door opened suddenly, and both men stopped talking at once.

Susan Calvin stepped in again, looking about uncertainly. "Have either of you seen—I'm positive I had it somewhere about—Oh, there it is."

She ran to a corner of one bookcase and picked up an object of intricate metal webbery, dumbbell shaped and hollow, with variously-shaped metal pieces inside each hollow, just too large to be able to fall out of the webbing.

As she picked it up, the metal pieces within moved and struck together, clicking pleasantly. It struck Lanning that the object was a kind of robotic version of a baby rattle.

As Susan Calvin opened the door again to pass through, Lenny's voice chimed again from within. This time, Lanning heard it clearly as it spoke the words Susan Calvin had taught it.

In heavenly celeste-like sounds, it called out, "Mommie, I want you. I want you, Mommie."

And the footsteps of Susan Calvin could be heard hurrying eagerly across the laboratory floor toward the only kind of baby she could ever have or love.

Galley Slave

The longest story involving Susan Calvin appeared in the December 1957 issue of Galaxy. *It came within a hair of not being written at all.*

Horace Gold, then editor of Galaxy, *called me long-distance to ask me to write a story for him—always a terribly flattering situation and with me flattery will get you everywhere.*

However, I had to explain regretfully that I was absolutely incapable of writing a story at the moment. I was deep in the galley proof of the third edition of a biochemistry textbook I was coauthoring.

"Can't you have someone else read the galley proof?" he asked.

"Of course not," I responded with virtuous indignation. "I couldn't trust these galleys to anyone else."

And having hung up, I walked upstairs to my beloved attic, galley proof in hand, and between the bottom step and the top step a thought occurred to me. I put the galleys to one side and got started at once. I continued at top speed until, a few days later, "Galley Slave" was done.

Of all my Susan Calvin stories, this is my favorite. I don't know that I can give a good reason for it; but then, I suppose an author may have his irrational likes and dislikes as well as the next man.

Galley Slave

The United States Robots and Mechanical Men, Inc., as defendants in the case, had influence enough to force a closed-doors trial without a jury.

Nor did Northeastern University try hard to prevent it. The trustees knew perfectly well how the public might react to any issue involving misbehavior of a robot, however rarefied that misbehavior might be. They also had a clearly visualized notion of how an antirobot riot might become an antiscience riot without warning.

The government, as represented in this case by Justice Harlow Shane, was equally anxious for a quiet end to this mess. Both U.S. Robots and the academic world were bad people to antagonize.

Justice Shane said, "Since neither press, public nor jury is present, gentlemen, let us stand on as little ceremony as we can and get to the facts."

He smiled stiffly as he said this, perhaps without much hope that his request would be effective, and hitched at his robe so that he might sit more comfortably. His face was pleasantly rubicund, his chin round and soft, his nose broad and his eyes light in color and wide-set. All in all, it was not a face with much judicial majesty and the judge knew it.

Barnabas H. Goodfellow, Professor of Physics at Northeastern U., was sworn in first, taking the usual vow with an expression that made mincemeat of his name.

After the usual opening-gambit questions, Prosecution shoved his hands deep into his pockets and said, "When was it, Professor, that the matter of the possible employ of Robot EZ-27 was first brought to your attention, and how?"

Professor Goodfellow's small and angular face set itself into an uneasy expression, scarcely more benevolent than the one it replaced. He said, "I have had professional contact and some social acquaintance with Dr. Alfred Lanning, Director of Research at U.S. Robots. I was inclined to listen with some tolerance then when I received a rather strange suggestion from him on the third of March of last year—"

"Of 2033?"

"That's right."

"Excuse me for interrupting. Please proceed."

The professor nodded frostily, scowled to fix the facts in his mind, and began to speak.

Professor Goodfellow looked at the robot with a certain uneasiness. It had been carried into the basement supply room in a crate, in accordance with the regulations governing the shipment of robots from place to place on the Earth's surface.

He knew it was coming; it wasn't that he was unprepared. From the moment of Dr. Lanning's first phone call on March 3, he had felt himself giving way to the other's persuasiveness, and now, as an inevitable result, he found himself face to face with a robot.

It looked uncommonly large as it stood within arm's reach.

Alfred Lanning cast a hard glance of his own at the robot, as though making certain it had not been damaged in transit. Then he turned his ferocious eyebrows and his mane of white hair in the professor's direction.

"This is Robot EZ-27, first of its model to be available for public use." He turned to the robot. "This is Professor Goodfellow, Easy."

Easy spoke impassively, but with such suddenness that the

professor shied. "Good afternoon, Professor."

Easy stood seven feet tall and had the general proportions of a man—always the prime selling point of U.S. Robots. That and the possession of the basic patents on the positronic brain had given them an actual monopoly on robots and a near-monopoly on computing machines in general.

The two men who had uncrated the robot had left now and the professor looked from Lanning to the robot and back to Lanning. "It is harmless, I'm sure." He didn't sound sure.

"More harmless than I am," said Lanning. "I could be goaded into striking you. Easy could not be. You know the Three Laws of Robotics, I presume."

"Yes, of course," said Goodfellow.

"They are built into the positronic patterns of the brain and must be observed. The First Law, the prime rule of robotic existence, safeguards the life and well-being of all humans." He paused, rubbed at his cheek, then added, "It's something of which we would like to persuade all Earth if we could."

"It's just that he seems formidable."

"Granted. But whatever he seems, you'll find that he *is* useful."

"I'm not sure in what way. Our conversations were not very helpful in that respect. Still, I agreed to look at the object and I'm doing it."

"We'll do more than look, Professor. Have you brought a book?"

"I have."

"May I see it?"

Professor Goodfellow reached down without actually taking his eyes off the metal-in-human-shape that confronted him. From the briefcase at his feet, he withdrew a book.

Lanning held out his hand for it and looked at the backstrip. *"Physical Chemistry of Electrolytes in Solution.* Fair enough, sir. You selected this yourself, at random. It was no suggestion of mine, this particular text. Am I right?"

"Yes."

Lanning passed the book to Robot EZ-27.

The professor jumped a little. "No! That's a valuable book!"

Lanning raised his eyebrows and they looked like shaggy coconut icing. He said, "Easy has no intention of tearing the book in two as a feat of strength, I assure you. It can handle a book as carefully as you or I. Go ahead, Easy."

"Thank you, sir," said Easy. Then, turning its metal bulk slightly, it added, "With your permission, Professor Goodfellow."

The professor stared, then said, "Yes—yes, of course."

With a slow and steady manipulation of metal fingers, Easy turned the pages of the book, glancing at the left page, then the right; turning the page, glancing left, then right; turning the page and so on for minute after minute.

The sense of its power seemed to dwarf even the large cement-walled room in which they stood and to reduce the two human watchers to something considerably less than life-size.

Goodfellow muttered, "The light isn't very good."

"It will do."

Then, rather more sharply, "But what is he doing?"

"Patience, sir."

The last page was turned eventually. Lanning asked, "Well, Easy?"

The robot said, "It is a most accurate book and there is little to which I can point. On line 22 of page 27, the word 'positive' is spelled p-o-i-s-t-i-v-e. The comma in line 6 of page 32 is superfluous, whereas one should have been used on line 13 of page 54. The plus sign in equation XIV-2 on page 337 should be a minus sign if it is to be consistent with the previous equation—"

"Wait! Wait!" cried the professor. "What is he doing?"

"Doing?" echoed Lanning in sudden irascibility. "Why, man, he has already done it! He has proofread that book."

"Proofread it?"

"Yes. In the short time it took him to turn those pages, he caught every mistake in spelling, grammar and punctuation. He has noted errors in word order and detected inconsistencies. And he will retain the information, letter-perfect, indefinitely."

The professor's mouth was open. He walked rapidly away from Lanning and Easy and as rapidly back. He folded his arms across his chest and stared at them. Finally he said, "You mean this is a proofreading robot?"

Lanning nodded. "Among other things."

"But why do you show it to me?"

"So that you might help me persuade the university to obtain it for use."

"To read proof?"

"Among other things," Lanning repeated patiently.

The professor drew his pinched face together in a kind of sour disbelief. "But this is ridiculous!"

"Why?"

"The university could never afford to buy this half-ton—it must weigh that at least—this half-ton proofreader."

"Proofreading is not all it will do. It will prepare reports from outlines, fill out forms, serve as an accurate memory-file, grade papers—"

"All picayune!"

Lanning said, "Not at all, as I can show you in a moment. But I think we can discuss this more comfortably in your office, if you have no objection."

"No, of course not," began the professor mechanically and took a half-step as though to turn. Then he snapped out, "But the robot—we can't take the robot. Really, Doctor, you'll have to crate it up again."

"Time enough. We can leave Easy here."

"Unattended?"

"Why not? He knows he is to stay. Professor Goodfellow, it is necessary to understand that a robot is far more reliable than a human being."

"I would be responsible for any damage—"

"There will be no damage. I guarantee that. Look, it's after hours. You expect no one here, I imagine, before tomorrow morning. The truck and my two men are outside. U.S. Robots will take any responsibility that may arise. None will. Call it a demonstration of the reliability of the robot."

The professor allowed himself to be led out of the storeroom. Nor did he look entirely comfortable in his own office, five stories up.

He dabbed at the line of droplets along the upper half of his forehead with a white handkerchief.

"As you know very well, Dr. Lanning, there are laws against the use of robots on Earth's surface," he pointed out.

"The laws, Professor Goodfellow, are not simple ones. Robots may not be used on public thoroughfares or within public edifices. They may not be used on private grounds or within private structures except under certain restrictions that usually turn out to be prohibitive. The university, however, is a large and privately owned institution that usually receives preferential treatment. If the robot is used only in a specific room for only academic purposes, if certain other restrictions are observed and if the men and women having occasion to enter the room cooperate fully, we may remain within the law."

"But all that trouble just to read proof?"

"The uses would be infinite, Professor. Robotic labor has so far been used only to relieve physical drudgery. Isn't there such a thing as mental drudgery? When a professor capable of the most useful creative thought is forced to spend two weeks painfully checking the spelling of lines of print and I offer you a machine that can do it in thirty minutes, is that picayune?"

"But the price—"

"The price need not bother you. You cannot buy EZ-27. U.S. Robots does not sell its products. But the university can lease EZ-27 for a thousand dollars a year—considerably less than the cost of a single microwave spectograph continuous-recording attachment."

Goodfellow looked stunned. Lanning followed up his advantage by saying, "I only ask that you put it up to whatever group makes the decisions here. I would be glad to speak to them if they want more information."

"Well," Goodfellow said doubtfully, "I can bring it up at next week's Senate meeting. I can't promise that will do any good, though."

"Naturally," said Lanning.

The Defense Attorney was short and stubby and carried himself rather portentously, a stance that had the effect of accentuating his double chin. He stared at Professor Goodfellow, once that witness had been handed over, and said, "You agreed rather readily, did you not?"

The Professor said briskly, "I suppose I was anxious to be rid of Dr. Lanning. I would have agreed to anything."

"With the intention of forgetting about it after he left?"

"Well—"

"Nevertheless, you did present the matter to a meeting of the Executive Board of the University Senate."

"Yes, I did."

"So that you agreed in good faith with Dr. Lanning's suggestions. You weren't just going along with a gag. You actually agreed enthusiastically, did you not?"

"I merely followed ordinary procedures."

"As a matter of fact, you weren't as upset about the robot as you now claim you were. You know the Three Laws of Robotics and you knew them at the time of your interview with Dr. Lanning."

"Well, yes."

"And you were perfectly willing to leave a robot at large and unattended."

"Dr. Lanning assured me—"

"Surely you would never have accepted his assurance if you had had the slightest doubt that the robot might be in the least dangerous."

The professor began frigidly, "I had every faith in the word—"

"That is all," said Defense abruptly.

As Professor Goodfellow, more than a bit ruffled, stood down, Justice Shane leaned forward and said, "Since I am not a robotics man myself, I would appreciate knowing precisely what the Three Laws of Robotics are. Would Dr. Lanning quote them for the benefit of the court?"

Dr. Lanning looked startled. He had been virtually bumping heads with the gray-haired woman at his side. He rose to his feet now and the woman looked up, too—expressionlessly.

Dr. Lanning said, "Very well, Your Honor." He paused as though about to launch into an oration and said, with laborious clarity, "First Law: a robot may not injure a human being, or, through inaction, allow a human being to come to harm. Second Law: a robot must obey the orders given it by human beings, except where such orders would conflict with the First Law. Third Law: a robot must protect its own existence as long as such protection does not conflict with the First or Second Laws."

"I see," said the judge, taking rapid notes. "These Laws are built into every robot, are they?"

"Into every one. That will be borne out by any roboticist."

"And into Robot EZ-27 specifically?"

"Yes, Your Honor."

"You will probably be required to repeat those statements under oath."

"I am ready to do so, Your Honor."

He sat down again.

Dr. Susan Calvin, robopsychologist-in-chief for U.S. Robots, who was the gray-haired woman sitting next to Lanning, looked at her titular superior without favor, but then she showed favor to no human being. She said, "Was Goodfellow's testimony accurate, Alfred?"

"Essentially," muttered Lanning. "He wasn't as nervous as all that about the robot and he was anxious enough to talk business with me when he heard the price. But there doesn't seem to be any drastic distortion."

Dr. Calvin said thoughtfully, "It might have been wise to put the price higher than a thousand."

"We were anxious to place Easy."

"I know. Too anxious, perhaps. They'll try to make it look as though we had an ulterior motive."

Lanning looked exasperated. "We did. I admitted that at the University Senate meeting."

"They can make it look as if we had one beyond the one we admitted."

Scott Robertson, son of the founder of U.S. Robots and still owner of a majority of the stock, leaned over from Dr. Calvin's other side and said in a kind of explosive whisper, "Why can't you get Easy to talk so we'll know where we're at?"

"You know he can't talk about it, Mr. Robertson."

"Make him. You're the psychologist, Dr. Calvin. *Make* him."

"If I'm the psychologist, Mr. Robertson," said Susan Calvin coldly, "let me make the decisions. My robot will not be *made* to do anything at the price of his well-being."

Robertson frowned and might have answered, but Justice Shane was tapping his gavel in a polite sort of way and they grudgingly fell silent.

Francis J. Hart, head of the Department of English and Dean of Graduate Studies, was on the stand. He was a plump man, meticulously dressed in dark clothing of a conservative cut, and possessing several strands of hair traversing the pink top of his cranium. He sat well back in the witness chair with his hands folded neatly in his lap and displaying, from time to time, a tight-lipped smile.

He said, "My first connection with the matter of the Robot EZ-27 was on the occasion of the session of the University Senate Executive Committee at which the subject was introduced by Professor Goodfellow. Thereafter, on the tenth of

April of last year, we held a special meeting on the subject, during which I was in the chair."

"Were minutes kept of the meeting of the Executive Committee? Of the special meeting, that is?"

"Well, no. It was a rather unusual meeting." The dean smiled briefly. "We thought it might remain confidential."

"What transpired at the meeting?"

Dean Hart was not entirely comfortable as chairman of that meeting. Nor did the other members assembled seem completely calm. Only Dr. Lanning appeared at peace with himself. His tall, gaunt figure and the shock of white hair that crowned him reminded Hart of portraits he had seen of Andrew Jackson.

Samples of the robot's work lay scattered along the central regions of the table and the reproduction of a graph drawn by the robot was now in the hands of Professor Minott of Physical Chemistry. The chemist's lips were pursed in obvious approval.

Hart cleared his throat and said, "There seems no doubt that the robot can perform certain routine tasks with adequate competence. I have gone over these, for instance, just before coming in and there is very little to find fault with."

He picked up a long sheet of printing, some three times as long as the average book page. It was a sheet of galley proof, designed to be corrected by authors before the type was set up in page form. Along both of the wide margins of the galley were proofmarks, neat and superbly legible. Occasionally, a word of print was crossed out and a new word substituted in the margin in characters so fine and regular it might easily have been print itself. Some of the corrections were blue to indicate the original mistake had been the author's, a few in red, where the printer had been wrong.

"Actually," said Lanning, "there is less than very little to find fault with. I should say there is nothing at all to find fault with, Dr. Hart. I'm sure the corrections are perfect, insofar as the original manuscript was. If the manuscript against which this galley was corrected was at fault in a matter of fact rather than of English, the robot is not competent to correct it."

"We accept that. However, the robot corrected word order on occasion and I don't think the rules of English are sufficiently hidebound for us to be sure that in each case the robot's choice was the correct one."

"Easy's positronic brain," said Lanning, showing large teeth as he smiled, "has been molded by the contents of all the standard works on the subject. I'm sure you cannot point to a case where the robot's choice was definitely the incorrect one."

Professor Minott looked up from the graph he still held. "The question in my mind, Dr. Lanning, is why we need a robot at all, with all the difficulties in public relations that would entail. The science of automation has surely reached the point where your company could design a machine, an ordinary computer of a type known and accepted by the public, that would correct galleys."

"I am sure we could," said Lanning stiffly, "but such a machine would require that the galleys be translated into special symbols or, at the least, transcribed on tapes. Any corrections would emerge in symbols. You would need to keep men employed translating words to symbols, symbols to words. Furthermore, such a computer could do no other job. It couldn't prepare the graph you hold in your hand, for instance."

Minott grunted.

Lanning went on. "The hallmark of the positronic robot is its flexibility. It can do a number of jobs. It is designed like a man so that it can use all the tools and machines that have, after all, been designed to be used by a man. It can talk to you and you can talk to it. You can actually reason with it up to a point. Compared to even a simple robot, an ordinary computer with a non-positronic brain is only a heavy adding machine."

Goodfellow looked up and said, "If we talk and reason with the robot, what are the chances of our confusing it? I suppose it doesn't have the capability of absorbing an infinite amount of data."

"No, it hasn't. But it should last five years with ordinary use. It will know when it will require clearing, and the company will do the job without charge."

"The *company* will?"

"Yes. The company reserves the right to service the robot outside the ordinary course of its duties. It is one reason we retain control of our positronic robots and lease rather than sell them. In the pursuit of its ordinary functions, any robot can be directed by any man. Outside its ordinary functions, a robot requires expert handling, and that we can give it. For instance, any of you might clear an EZ robot to an extent by telling it to forget this item or that. But you would be almost certain to phrase the order in such a way as to cause it to forget too much or too little. We would detect such tampering, because we have built-in safeguards. However, since there is no need for clearing the robot in its ordinary work, or for doing other useless things, this raises no problem."

Dean Hart touched his head as though to make sure his carefully cultivated strands lay evenly distributed and said, "You are anxious to have us take the machine. Yet surely it is a losing proposition for U.S. Robots. One thousand a year is a ridiculously low price. Is it that you hope through this to rent other such machines to other universities at a more reasonable price?"

"Certainly that's a fair hope," said Lanning.

"But even so, the number of machines you could rent would be limited. I doubt if you could make it a paying proposition."

Lanning put his elbows on the table and earnestly leaned forward. "Let me put it bluntly, gentlemen. Robots cannot be used on Earth, except in certain special cases, because of prejudice against them on the part of the public. U.S. Robots is a highly successful corporation with our extraterrestrial and space-flight markets alone, to say nothing of our computer subsidiaries. However, we are concerned with more than profits alone. It is our firm belief that the use of robots on Earth itself would mean a better life for all eventually, even if a certain amount of economic dislocation resulted at first.

"The labor unions are naturally against us, but surely we may expect cooperation from the large universities. The robot, Easy, will help you by relieving you of scholastic drudgery— by assuming, if you permit it, the role of galley slave for you. Other universities and research institutions will follow your lead, and if it works out, then perhaps other robots of other types may be placed and the public's objections to them broken down by stages."

Minott murmured, "Today Northeastern University, tomorrow the world."

Angrily, Lanning whispered to Susan Calvin, "I wasn't nearly that eloquent and they weren't nearly that reluctant. At a thousand a year, they were jumping to get Easy. Professor Minott told me he'd never seen as beautiful a job as that graph he was holding and there was no mistake on the galley or anywhere else. Hart admitted it freely."

The severe vertical lines on Dr. Calvin's face did not soften. "You should have demanded more money than they could pay, Alfred, and let them beat you down."

"Maybe," he grumbled.

Prosecution was not quite done with Professor Hart. "After Dr. Lanning left, did you vote on whether to accept Robot EZ-27?"

"Yes, we did."

"With what result?"

"In favor of acceptance, by majority vote."

"What would you say influenced the vote?"

Defense objected immediately.

Prosecution rephrased the question. "What influenced you, personally, in your individual vote? You did vote in favor, I think."

"I voted in favor, yes. I did so largely because I was impressed by Dr. Lanning's feeling that it was our duty as members of the world's intellectual leadership to allow robotics to help Man in the solution of his problems."

"In other words, Dr. Lanning talked you into it."

"That's his job. He did it very well."

"Your witness."

Defense strode up to the witness chair and surveyed Professor Hart for a long moment. He said, "In reality, you were all pretty eager to have Robot EZ-27 in your employ, weren't you?"

"We thought that if it could do the work, it might be useful."

"*If* it could do the work? I understand you examined the samples of Robot EZ-27's original work with particular care on the day of the meeting which you have just described."

"Yes, I did. Since the machine's work dealt primarily with the handling of the English language, and since that is my field of competence, it seemed logical that I be the one chosen to examine the work."

"Very good. Was there anything on display on the table at the time of the meeting which was less than satisfactory? I have all the material here as exhibits. Can you point to a single unsatisfactory item?"

"Well—"

"It's a simple question. Was there one single solitary unsatisfactory item? You inspected it. Was there?"

The English professor frowned. "There wasn't."

"I also have some samples of work done by Robot EZ-27 during the course of his fourteen-month employ at Northeastern. Would you examine these and tell me if there is anything wrong with them in even one particular?"

Hart snapped, "When he did make a mistake, it was a beauty."

"Answer my question," thundered Defense, "and only the question I am putting to you! Is there anything wrong with the material?"

Dean Hart looked cautiously at each item. "Well, nothing."

"Barring the matter concerning which we are here engaged, do you know of any mistake on the part of EZ-27?"

"Barring the matter for which this trial is being held, no."

Defense cleared his throat as though to signal end of paragraph. He said, "Now about the vote concerning whether Robot EZ-27 was to be employed or not. You said there was a majority in favor. What was the actual vote?"

"Thirteen to one, as I remember."

"Thirteen to one! More than just a majority, wouldn't you say?"

"No sir!" All the pedant in Dean Hart was aroused. "In the English language, the word 'majority' means 'more than half.' Thirteen out of fourteen is a majority, nothing more."

"But an almost unanimous one."

"A majority all the same!"

Defense switched ground. "And who was the lone holdout?"

Dean Hart looked acutely uncomfortable. "Professor Simon Ninheimer."

Defense pretended astonishment. "Professor Ninheimer? The head of the Department of Sociology?"

"Yes, sir."

"The *plaintiff?*"

"Yes, sir."

Defense pursed his lips. "In other words, it turns out that the man bringing the action for payment of $750,000 damages against my client, United States Robots and Mechanical Men, Incorporated, was the one who from the beginning opposed

the use of the robot—although everyone else on the Executive
Committee of the University Senate was persuaded that it was
a good idea."

"He voted against the motion, as was his right."

"You didn't mention in your description of the meeting any
remarks made by Professor Ninheimer. Did he make any?"

"I think he spoke."

"You *think?*"

"Well, he *did* speak."

"Against using the robot?"

"Yes."

"Was he violent about it?"

Dean Hart paused. "He was vehement."

Defense grew confidential. "How long have you known
Professor Ninheimer, Dean Hart?"

"About twelve years."

"Reasonably well?"

"I should say so, yes."

"Knowing him, then, would you say he was the kind of
man who might continue to bear resentment against a robot,
all the more so because an adverse vote had—"

Prosecution drowned out the remainder of the question with
an indignant and vehement objection of his own. Defense motioned the witness down and Justice Shane called luncheon
recess.

Robertson mangled his sandwich. The corporation would not
founder for loss of three-quarters of a million, but the loss
would do it no particular good. He was conscious, moreover,
that there would be a much more costly long-term setback in
public relations.

He said sourly, "Why all this business about how Easy got
into the university? What do they hope to gain?"

The Attorney for Defense said quietly, "A court action is
like a chess game, Mr. Robertson. The winner is usually the
one who can see more moves ahead, and my friend at the
prosecutor's table is no beginner. They can show damage; that's
no problem. Their main effort lies in anticipating our defense.
They must be counting on us to try to show that Easy couldn't
possibly have committed the offense—because of the Laws of
Robotics."

"All right," said Robertson, "that *is* our defense. An absolutely airtight one."

"To a robotics engineer. Not necessarily to a judge. They're setting themselves up a position from which they can demonstrate that EZ-27 was no ordinary robot. It was the first of its type to be offered to the public. It was an experimental model that needed field-testing and the university was the only decent way to provide such testing. That would look plausible in the light of Dr. Lanning's strong efforts to place the robot and the willingness of U.S. Robots to lease it for so little. The prosecution would then argue that the field test proved Easy to have been a failure. Now do you see the purpose of what's been going on?"

"But EZ-27 was a perfectly good model," argued Robertson. "It was the twenty-seventh in production."

"Which is really a bad point," said Defense somberly. "What was wrong with the first twenty-six? Obviously something. Why shouldn't there be something wrong with the twenty-seventh, too?"

"There was nothing wrong with the first twenty-six except that they weren't complex enough for the task. These were the first positronic brains of the sort to be constructed and it was rather hit-and-miss to begin with. But the Three Laws held in all of them! *No* robot is so imperfect that the Three Laws don't hold."

"Dr. Lanning has explained this to me, Mr. Robertson, and I am willing to take his word for it. The judge, however, may not be. We are expecting a decision from an honest and intelligent man who knows no robotics and thus may be led astray. For instance, if you or Dr. Lanning or Dr. Calvin were to say on the stand that any positronic brains were constructed 'hit-and-miss,' as you just did, prosecution would tear you apart in cross-examination. Nothing would salvage our case. So that's something to avoid."

Robertson growled, "If only Easy would talk."

Defense shrugged. "A robot is incompetent as a witness, so that would do us no good."

"At least we'd know some of the facts. We'd know how it came to do such a thing."

Susan Calvin fired up. A dullish red touched her cheeks and her voice had a trace of warmth in it. "We *know* how Easy came to do it. It was ordered to! I've explained this to counsel and I'll explain it to you now."

"Ordered to by whom?" asked Robertson in honest astonishment. (No one ever told him anything, he thought resentfully. These research people considered *themselves* the owners of U.S. Robots, by God!)

"By the plaintiff," said Dr. Calvin.

"In heaven's name, why?"

"I don't know why yet. Perhaps just that we might be sued, that he might gain some cash." There were blue glints in her eyes as she said that.

"Then why doesn't Easy say so?"

"Isn't that obvious? It's been ordered to keep quiet about the matter."

"Why should that be obvious?" demanded Robertson truculently.

"Well, it's obvious to me. Robot psychology is my profession. If Easy will not answer questions about the matter directly, he will answer questions on the fringe of the matter. By measuring increased hesitation in his answers as the central question is approached, by measuring the area of blankness and the intensity of counterpotentials set up, it is possible to tell with scientific precision that his troubles are the result of an order not to talk, with its strength based on First Law. In other words, he's been told that if he talks, harm will be done a human being. Presumably harm to the unspeakable Professor Ninheimer, the plaintiff, who, to the robot, would seem a human being."

"Well, then," said Robertson, "can't you explain that if he keeps quiet, harm will be done to U.S. Robots?"

"U.S. Robots is not a human being and the First Law of Robotics does not recognize a corporation as a person the way ordinary laws do. Besides, it would be dangerous to try to lift this particular sort of inhibition. The person who laid it on could lift it off least dangerously, because the robot's motivations in that respect are centered on that person. Any other course—" She shook her head and grew almost impassioned. "I won't let the robot be damaged!" Lanning interrupted with the air of bringing sanity to the problem. "It seems to me that we have only to prove a robot incapable of the act of which Easy is accused. We can do that."

"Exactly," said Defense, in annoyance. "*You* can do that.

The only witnesses capable of testifying to Easy's condition and the nature of Easy's state of mind are employees of U.S. Robots. The judge can't possibly accept their testimony as unprejudiced."

"How can he deny expert testimony?"

"By refusing to be convinced by it. That's his right as the judge. Against the alternative that a man like Professor Ninheimer deliberately set about ruining his own reputation, even for a sizable sum of money, the judge isn't going to accept the technicalities of your engineers. The judge is a man, after all. If he has to choose between a man doing an impossible thing and a robot doing an impossible thing, he's quite likely to decide in favor of the man."

"A man *can* do an impossible thing," said Lanning, "because we don't know all the complexities of the human mind and we don't know what, in a given human mind, is impossible and what is not. We *do* know what is really impossible to a robot."

"Well, we'll see if we can't convince the judge of that," Defense replied wearily.

"If all you say is so," rumbled Robertson, "I don't see how you can."

"We'll see. It's good to know and be aware of the difficulties involved, but let's not be *too* downhearted. I've tried to look ahead a few moves in the chess game, too." With a stately nod in the direction of the robopsychologist, he added, *"With* the help of the good lady here."

Lanning looked from one to the other and said, "What the devil is this?"

But the bailiff thrust his head into the room and announced somewhat breathlessly that the trial was about to resume.

They took their seats, examining the man who had started all the trouble.

Simon Ninheimer owned a fluffy head of sandy hair, a face that narrowed past a beaked nose toward a pointed chin, and a habit of sometimes hesitating before key words in his conversation that gave him an air of a seeker after an almost unbearable precision. When he said, "The Sun rises in the—uh—east," one was certain he had given due consideration to the possibility that it might at some time rise in the west.

Prosecution said, "Did you oppose employment of Robot EZ-27 by the university?"

"I did, sir."

"Why was that?"

"I did not feel that we understood the—uh—motives of U.S. Robots thoroughly. I mistrusted their anxiety to place the robot with us."

"Did you feel that it was capable of doing the work that it was allegedly designed to do?"

"I know for a fact that it was not."

"Would you state your reasons?"

Simon Ninheimer's book, entitled *Social Tensions Involved in Space-Flight and Their Resolution,* had been eight years in the making. Ninheimer's search for precision was not confined to his habits of speech, and in a subject like sociology, almost inherently imprecise, it left him breathless.

Even with the material in galley proofs, he felt no sense of completion. Rather the reverse, in fact. Staring at the long strips of print, he felt only the itch to tear the lines of type apart and rearrange them differently.

Jim Baker, Instructor and soon to be Assistant Professor of Sociology, found Ninheimer, three days after the first batch of galleys had arrived from the printer, staring at the handful of paper in abstraction. The galleys came in three copies: one for Ninheimer to proofread, one for Baker to proofread independently, and a third, marked "Original," which was to receive the final corrections, a combination of those made by Ninheimer and by Baker, after a conference at which possible conflicts and disagreements were ironed out. This had been their policy on the several papers on which they had collaborated in the past three years and it worked well.

Baker, young and ingratiatingly soft-voiced, had his own copies of the galleys in his hand. He said eagerly, "I've done the first chapter and they contain some typographical beauts."

"The first chapter always has them," said Ninheimer distantly.

"Do you want to go over it now?"

Ninheimer brought his eyes to grave focus on Baker. "I haven't done anything on the galleys, Jim. I don't think I'll bother."

Baker looked confused. "Not bother?"

Ninheimer pursed his lips. "I've asked about the—uh—

workload of the machine. After all, he was originally—uh—
promoted as a proofreader. They've set a schedule." ·

"The *machine?* You mean Easy?"

"I believe that is the foolish name they gave it."

"But, Dr. Ninheimer, I thought you were staying clear of
it!"

"I seem to be the only one doing so. Perhaps I ought to
take my share of the—uh—advantage."

"Oh. Well, I seem to have wasted time on this first chapter,
then," said the younger man ruefully.

"Not wasted. We can compare the machine's result with
yours as a check."

"If you want to, but—"

"Yes?"

"I doubt that we'll find anything wrong with Easy's work.
It's supposed never to have made a mistake."

"I dare say," said Ninheimer dryly.

The first chapter was brought in again by Baker four days later.
This time it was Ninheimer's copy, fresh from the special annex
that had been built to house Easy and the equipment it used.

Baker was jubilant. "Dr. Ninheimer, it not only caught
everything I caught—it found a dozen errors I missed! The
whole thing took it twelve minutes!"

Ninheimer looked over the sheaf, with the neatly printed
marks and symbols in the margins. He said, "It is not as complete as you and I would have made it. We would have entered
an insert on Suzuki's work on the neurological effects of low
gravity."

"You mean his paper in *Sociological Reviews?*"

"Of course."

"Well, you can't expect impossibilities of Easy. It can't
read the literature for us."

"I realize that. As a matter of fact, I have prepared the
insert. I will see the machine and make certain it knows how
to—uh—handle inserts."

"It will know."

"I prefer to make certain."

Ninheimer had to make an appointment to see Easy, and
then could get nothing better than fifteen minutes in the late
evening.

But the fifteen minutes turned out to be ample. Robot EZ-27 understood the matter of inserts at once.

Ninheimer found himself uncomfortable at close quarters with the robot for the first time. Almost automatically, as though it were human, he found himself asking, "Are you happy with your work?"

"Most happy, Professor Ninheimer," said Easy solemnly, the photocells that were its eyes gleaming their normal deep red.

"You know me?"

"From the fact that you present me with additional material to include in the galleys, it follows that you are the author. The author's name, of course, is at the head of each sheet of galley proof."

"I see. You make—uh—deductions, then. Tell me—" he couldn't resist the question—"what do you think of the book so far?"

Easy said, "I find it very pleasant to work with."

"Pleasant? That is an odd word for a—uh—a mechanism without emotion. I've been told you have no emotion."

"The words of your book go in accordance with my circuits," Easy explained. "They set up little or no counter-potentials. It is in my brain-paths to translate this mechanical fact into a word such as 'pleasant.' The emotional context is fortuitous."

"I see. Why do you find the book pleasant?"

"It deals with human beings, Professor, and not with in-organic materials or mathematical symbols. Your book attempts to understand human beings and to help increase human happiness."

"And this is what you try to do and so my book goes in accordance with your circuits? Is that it?"

"That is it, Professor."

The fifteen minutes were up. Ninheimer left and went to the university library, which was on the point of closing. He kept them open long enough to find an elementary text on robotics. He took it home with him.

Except for occasional insertion of late material, the galleys went to Easy and from him to the publishers with little intervention from Ninheimer at first—and none at all later.

Baker said, a little uneasily, "It almost gives me a feeling of uselessness."

"It should give you a feeling of having time to begin a new

project," said Ninheimer, without looking up from the notations he was making in the current issue of *Social Science Abstracts*.

"I'm just not used to it. I keep worrying about the galleys. It's silly, I know."

"It is."

"The other day I got a couple of sheets before Easy sent them off to—"

"What!" Ninheimer looked up, scowling. The copy of *Abstracts* slid shut. "Did you disturb the machine at its work?"

"Only for a minute. Everything was all right. Oh, it changed one word. You referred to something as 'criminal'; it changed the word to 'reckless.' It thought the second adjective fit in better with the context."

Ninheimer turned in his swivel-chair to face his young associate. "See here, I wish you wouldn't do this again. If I am to use the machine, I wish the—uh—full advantage of it. If I am to use it and lose your—uh—services anyway because you supervise it when the whole point is that it requires no supervision, I gain nothing. Do you see?"

"Yes, Dr. Ninheimer," said Baker, subdued.

The advance copies of *Social Tensions* arrived in Dr. Ninheimer's office on the eighth of May. He looked through it briefly, flipping pages and pausing to read a paragraph here and there. Then he put his copies away.

As he explained later, he forgot about it. For eight years, he had worked at it, but now, and for months in the past, other interests had engaged him while Easy had taken the load of the book off his shoulders. He did not even think to donate the usual complimentary copy to the university library. Even Baker, who had thrown himself into work and had steered clear of the department head since receiving his rebuke at their last meeting, received no copy.

On the sixteenth of June that stage ended. Ninheimer received a phone call and stared at the image in the 'plate with surprise.

"Speidell! Are you in town?"

"No, sir. I'm in Cleveland." Speidell's voice trembled with emotion.

"Then why the call?"

"Because I've just been looking through your new book! Ninheimer, are you *mad*? Have you gone *insane*?"

• • •

Ninheimer stiffened, "Is something—uh—wrong?" he asked in alarm.

"Wrong? I refer you to page 562. What in blazes do you mean by interpreting my work as you do? Where in the paper cited do I make the claim that the criminal personality is non-existent and that it is the *law*-enforcement agencies that are the *true* criminals? Here, let me quote—"

"Wait! Wait!" cried Ninheimer, trying to find the page. "Let me see. Let me see . . . Good God!"

"Well?"

"Speidell, I don't see how this could have happened. I never wrote this."

"But that's what's printed! And that distortion isn't the worst. You look at page 690 and imagine what Ipatiev is going to do to you when he sees the hash you've made of his findings! Look, Ninheimer, the book is *riddled* with this sort of thing. I don't know what you were thinking of—but there's nothing to do but get the book off the market. And you'd better be prepared for extensive apologies at the next Association meeting!"

"Speidell, listen to me—"

But Speidell had flashed off with a force that had the 'plate glowing with after-images for fifteen seconds.

It was then that Ninheimer went through the book and began marking off passages with red ink.

He kept his temper remarkably well when he faced Easy again, but his lips were pale. He passed the book to Easy and said, "Will you read the marked passages on pages 562, 631, 664 and 690?"

Easy did so in four glances. "Yes, Professor Ninheimer."

"This is not as I had it in the original galleys."

"No, sir. It is not."

"Did you change it to read as it now does?"

"Yes, sir."

"Why?"

"Sir, the passages as they read in your version were most uncomplimentary to certain groups of human beings. I felt it advisable to change the wording to avoid doing them harm."

"How *dared* you do such a thing?"

"The First Law, Professor, does not let me, through any inaction, allow harm to come to human beings. Certainly, considering your reputation in the world of sociology and the wide circulation your book would receive among scholars, considerable harm would come to a number of the human beings you speak of."

"But do you realize the harm that will come to *me* now?"

"It was necessary to choose the alternative with less harm."

Professor Ninheimer, shaking with fury, staggered away. It was clear to him that U.S. Robots would have to account to him for this.

There was some excitement at the defendants' table, which increased as Prosecution drove the point home.

"Then Robot EZ-27 informed you that the reason for its action was based on the First Law of Robotics?"

"That is correct, sir."

"That, in effect, it had no choice?"

"Yes, sir."

"It follows then that U.S. Robots designed a robot that would of necessity rewrite books to accord with its own conceptions of what was right. And yet they palmed it off as a simple proofreader. Would you say that?"

Defense objected firmly at once, pointing out that the witness was being asked for a decision on a matter in which he had no competence. The judge admonished Prosecution in the usual terms, but there was no doubt that the exchange had sunk home—not least upon the attorney for the Defense.

Defense asked for a short recess before beginning cross-examination, using a legal technicality for the purpose that got him five minutes.

He leaned over toward Susan Calvin. "Is it possible, Dr. Calvin, that Professor Ninheimer is telling the truth and that Easy was motivated by the First Law?"

Calvin pressed her lips together, then said, "No. It *isn't* possible. The last part of Ninheimer's testimony is deliberate perjury. Easy is not designed to be able to judge matters at the stage of abstraction represented by an advanced textbook on sociology. It would never be able to tell that certain groups of humans would be harmed by a phrase in such a book. Its mind is simply not built for that."

"I suppose, though, that we can't prove this to a layman," said Defense pessimistically.

"No," admitted Calvin. "The proof would be highly complex. Our way out is still what it was. We must prove Ninheimer is lying, and nothing he has said need change our plan of attack."

"Very well, Dr. Calvin," said Defense, "I must accept your word in this. We'll go on as planned."

In the courtroom, the judge's gavel rose and fell and Dr. Ninheimer took the stand once more. He smiled a little as one who feels his position to be impregnable and rather enjoys the prospect of countering a useless attack.

Defense approached warily and began softly. "Dr. Ninheimer, do you mean to say that you were completely unaware of these alleged changes in your manuscript until such time as Dr. Speidell called you on the sixteenth of June?"

"That is correct, sir."

"Did you never look at the galleys after Robot EZ-27 had proofread them?"

"At first I did, but it seemed to me a useless task. I relied on the claims of U.S. Robots. The absurd—uh—changes were made only in the last quarter of the book after the robot, I presume, had learned enough about sociology—"

"Never mind your presumptions!" said Defense. "I understood your colleague, Dr. Baker, saw the later galleys on at least one occasion. Do you remember testifying to that effect?"

"Yes, sir. As I said, he told me about seeing one page, and even there, the robot had changed a word."

Again Defense broke in. "Don't you find it strange, sir, that after over a year of implacable hostility to the robot, after having voted against it in the first place and having refused to put it to any use whatever, you suddenly decided to put your book, your *magnum opus*, into its hands?"

"I don't find that strange. I simply decided that I might as well use the machine."

"And you were so confident of Robot EZ-27—all of a sudden—that you didn't even bother to check your galleys?"

"I told you I was—uh—persuaded by U.S. Robots' propaganda."

"So persuaded that when your colleague, Dr. Baker, attempted to check on the robot, you berated him soundly?"

"I didn't berate him. I merely did not wish to have him—

uh—waste his time. At least, I thought then it was a waste of time. I did not see the significance of that change in a word at the—"

Defense said with heavy sarcasm, "I have no doubt you were instructed to bring up that point in order that the word-change be entered in the record—" He altered his line to forestall objection and said, "The point is that you were extremely angry with Dr. Baker."

"No, sir. Not angry."

"You didn't give him a copy of your book when you received it."

"Simple forgetfulness. I didn't give the library its copy, either." Ninheimer smiled cautiously. "Professors are notoriously absent-minded."

Defense said, "Do you find it strange that, after more than a year of perfect work, Robot EZ-27 should go wrong on your book? On a book, that is, which was written by you, who was, of all people, the most implacably hostile to the robot?"

"My book was the only sizable work dealing with mankind that it had to face. The Three Laws of Robotics took hold then."

"Several times, Dr. Ninheimer," said Defense, "you have tried to sound like an expert on robotics. Apparently you suddenly grew interested in robotics and took out books on the subject from the library. You testified to that effect, did you not?"

"One book, sir. That was the result of what seems to me to have been—uh—natural curiosity."

"And it enabled you to explain why the robot should, as you allege, have distorted your book?"

"Yes, sir."

"Very convenient. But are you sure your interest in robotics was not intended to enable you to manipulate the robot for your own purposes?"

Ninheimer flushed. "Certainly not, sir!"

Defense's voice rose. "In fact, are you sure the alleged altered passages were not as you had them in the first place?"

The sociologist half-rose. "That's—uh—uh—ridiculous! I have the galleys—"

He had difficulty speaking and Prosecution rose to insert smoothly, "With your permission, Your Honor, I intend to introduce as evidence the set of galleys given by Dr. Ninheimer to Robot EZ-27 and the set of galleys mailed by Robot EZ-27 to the publishers. I will do so now if my esteemed colleague so desires, and will be willing to allow a recess in order that the two sets of galleys may be compared."

Defense waved his hand impatiently. "That is not necessary. My honored opponent can introduce those galleys whenever he chooses. I'm sure they will show whatever discrepancies are claimed by the plaintiff to exist. What I would like to know of the witness, however, is whether he also has in his possession Dr. *Baker's* galleys."

"Dr. Baker's galleys?" Ninheimer frowned. He was not yet quite master of himself.

"Yes, Professor! I mean Dr. Baker's galleys. You testified to the effect that Dr. Baker had received a separate copy of the galleys. I will have the clerk read your testimony if you are suddenly a selective type of amnesiac. Or is it just that professors are, as you say, notoriously absent-minded?"

Ninheimer said, "I remember Dr. Baker's galleys. They weren't necessary once the job was placed in the care of the proofreading machine—"

"So you burned them?"

"No. I put them in the wastebasket."

"Burned them, dumped them—what's the difference? The point is you got rid of them."

"There's nothing wrong—" began Ninheimer weakly.

"Nothing wrong?" thundered Defense. "Nothing wrong except that there is now no way we can check to see if, on certain crucial galley sheets, you might not have substituted a harmless blank one from Dr. Baker's copy for a sheet in your own copy which you had deliberately mangled in such a way as to force the robot to—"

Prosecution shouted a furious objection. Justice Shane leaned forward, his round face doing its best to assume an expression of anger equivalent to the intensity of the emotion felt by the man.

The judge said, "Do you have any evidence, Counselor, for the extraordinary statement you have just made?"

Defense said quietly, "No direct evidence, Your Honor. But I would like to point out that, viewed properly, the sudden conversion of the plaintiff from anti-roboticism, his sudden interest in robotics, his refusal to check the galleys or to allow anyone else to check them, his careful neglect to allow anyone to see the book immediately after publication, all very clearly point—"

"Counselor," interrupted the judge impatiently, "this is not the place for esoteric deductions. The plaintiff is not on trial. Neither are you prosecuting him. I forbid this line of attack and I can only point out that the desperation that must have induced you to do this cannot help but weaken your case. If you have legitimate questions to ask, Counselor, you may continue with your cross-examination. But I warn you against another such exhibition in this courtroom."

"I have no further questions, Your Honor."

Robertson whispered heatedly as counsel for the Defense returned to his table, "What good did that do, for God's sake? The judge is dead-set against you now."

Defense replied calmly, "But Ninheimer is good and rattled. And we've set him up for tomorrow's move. He'll be ripe."

Susan Calvin nodded gravely.

The rest of Prosecution's case was mild in comparison. Dr. Baker was called and bore out most of Ninheimer's testimony. Drs. Speidell and Ipatiev were called, and they expounded most movingly on their shock and dismay at certain quoted passages in Dr. Ninheimer's book. Both gave their professional opinion that Dr. Ninheimer's professional reputation had been seriously impaired.

The galleys were introduced in evidence, as were copies of the finished book.

Defense cross-examined no more that day. Prosecution rested and the trial was recessed till the next morning.

Defense made his first motion at the beginning of the proceedings on the second day. He requested that Robot EZ-27 be admitted as a spectator to the proceedings.

Prosecution objected at once and Justice Shane called both to the bench.

Prosecution said hotly, "This is obviously illegal. A robot may not be in any edifice used by the general public."

"This courtroom," pointed out Defense, "is closed to all but those having an immediate connection with the case."

"A large machine of *known* erratic behavior would disturb my clients and my witnesses by its very presence! It would make hash out of the proceedings."

The judge seemed inclined to agree. He turned to Defense and said rather unsympathetically, "What are the reasons for your request?"

Defense said, "It will be our contention that Robot EZ-27 could not possibly, by the nature of its construction, have behaved as it has been described as behaving. It will be necessary to present a few demonstrations."

Prosecution said, "I don't see the point, Your Honor. Demonstrations conducted by men employed at U.S. Robots are worth little as evidence when U.S. Robots is the defendant."

"Your Honor," said Defense, "the validity of any evidence is for you to decide, not for the Prosecuting Attorney. At least, that is my understanding."

Justice Shane, his prerogatives encroached upon, said, "Your understanding is correct. Nevertheless, the presence of a robot here does raise important legal questions."

"Surely, Your Honor, nothing about that should be allowed to override the requirements of justice. If the robot is not present, we are prevented from presenting our only defense."

The judge considered. "There would be the question of transporting the robot here."

"That is a problem with which U.S. Robots has frequently been faced. We have a truck parked outside the courtroom, constructed according to the laws governing the transportation of robots. Robot EZ-27 is in a packing case inside with two men guarding it. The doors to the truck are properly secured and all other necessary precautions have been taken."

"You seem certain," said Justice Shane, in renewed illtemper, "that judgment on this point will be in your favor."

"Not at all, Your Honor. If it is not, we simply turn the truck about. I have made no presumptions concerning your decision."

The judge nodded. "The request on the part of the Defense is granted."

The crate was carried in on a large dolly and the two men who handled it opened it. The courtroom was immersed in a dead silence.

• • •

Susan Calvin waited as the thick slabs of celluform went down, then held out one hand. "Come, Easy."

The robot looked in her direction and held out its large metal arm. It towered over her by two feet but followed meekly, like a child in the clasp of its mother. Someone giggled nervously and choked it off at a hard glare from Dr. Calvin.

Easy seated itself carefully in a large chair brought by the bailiff, which creaked but held.

Defense said, "When it becomes necessary, Your Honor, we will prove that this is actually Robot EZ-27, the specific robot in the employ of Northeastern University during the period of time with which we are concerned."

"Good," His Honor said. "That will be necessary. I, for one, have no idea how you can tell one robot from another."

"And now," said Defense, "I would like to call my first witness to the stand. Professor Simon Ninheimer, please."

The clerk hesitated, looked at the judge. Justice Shane asked, with visible surprise, "You are calling the *plaintiff* as your witness?"

"Yes, Your Honor."

"I hope that you're aware that as long as he's your witness, you will be allowed none of the latitude you might exercise if you were cross-examining an opposing witness."

Defense said smoothly, "My only purpose in all this is to arrive at the truth. It will not be necessary to do more than ask a few polite questions."

"Well," said the judge dubiously, "you're the one handling the case. Call the witness."

Ninheimer took the stand and was informed that he was still under oath. He looked more nervous than he had the day before, almost apprehensive.

But Defense looked at him benignly.

"Now, Professor Ninheimer, you are suing my clients in the amount of $750,000."

"That is the—uh—sum. Yes."

"That is a great deal of money."

"I have suffered a great deal of harm."

"Surely not that much. The material in question involves only a few passages in a book. Perhaps these were unfortunate passages, but after all, books sometimes appear with curious mistakes in them."

Ninheimer's nostrils flared. "Sir, this book was to have been the climax of my professional career! Instead, it makes me look like an incompetent scholar, a perverter of the views held by my honored friends and associates, and a believer of ridiculous and—uh—outmoded viewpoints. My reputation is irretrievably shattered! I can never hold up my head in any—uh—assemblage of scholars, regardless of the outcome of this trial. I certainly cannot continue in my career, which has been the whole of my life. The very purpose of my life has been—uh—aborted and destroyed."

Defense made no attempt to interrupt the speech, but stared abstractedly at his fingernails as it went on.

He said very soothingly, "But surely, Professor Ninheimer, at your present age, you could not hope to earn more than—let us be generous—$150,000 during the remainder of your life. Yet you are asking the court to award you five times as much."

Ninheimer said, with an even greater burst of emotion, "It is not in my lifetime alone that I am ruined. I do not know for how many generations I shall be pointed at by sociologists as a—uh—a fool or maniac. My real achievements will be buried and ignored. I am ruined not only until the day of my death, but for all time to come, because there will always be people who will not believe that a robot made those insertions—"

It was at this point that Robot EZ-27 rose to his feet. Susan Calvin made no move to stop him. She sat motionless, staring straight ahead. Defense sighed softly.

Easy's melodious voice carried clearly. It said, "I would like to explain to everyone that I did insert certain passages in the galley proofs that seemed directly opposed to what had been there at first—"

Even the Prosecuting Attorney was too startled at the spectacle of a seven-foot robot rising to address the court to be able to demand the stopping of what was obviously a most irregular procedure.

When he could collect his wits, it was too late. For Ninheimer rose in the witness chair, his face working.

He shouted wildly, "Damn you, you were instructed to keep your mouth shut about—"

He ground to a choking halt, and Easy was silent, too.

Prosecution was on his feet now, demanding that a mistrial be declared.

Justice Shane banged his gavel desperately. "Silence! Silence! Certainly there is every reason here to declare a mistrial, except that in the interests of justice I would like to have Professor Ninheimer complete his statement. I distinctly heard him say to the robot that the robot had been instructed to keep its mouth shut about something. There was no mention in your testimony, Professor Ninheimer, as to any instructions to the robot to keep silent about anything!"

Ninheimer stared wordlessly at the judge.

Justice Shane said, "Did you instruct Robot EZ-27 to keep silent about something? And if so, about what?"

"Your Honor—" began Ninheimer hoarsely, and couldn't continue.

The judge's voice grew sharp. "Did you, in fact, order the inserts in question to be made in the galleys and then order the robot to keep quiet about your part in this?"

Prosecution objected vigorously, but Ninheimer shouted, "Oh, what's the use? Yes!" And he ran from the witness stand. He was stopped at the door by the bailiff and sank hopelessly into one of the last rows of seats, head buried in both hands.

Justice Shane said, "It is evident to me that Robot EZ-27 was brought here as a trick. Except for the fact that the trick served to prevent a serious miscarriage of justice, I would certainly hold attorney for the Defense in contempt. It is clear now, beyond any doubt, that the plaintiff has committed what is to me a completely inexplicable fraud since, apparently, he was knowingly ruining his career in the process—"

Judgment, of course, was for the defendant.

Dr. Susan Calvin had herself announced at Dr. Ninheimer's bachelor quarters in University Hall. The young engineer who had driven the car offered to go up with her, but she looked at him scornfully.

"Do you think he'll assault me? Wait down here."

Ninheimer was in no mood to assault anyone. He was packing, wasting no time, anxious to be away before the adverse conclusion of the trial became general knowledge.

He looked at Calvin with a queerly defiant air and said, "Are you coming to warn me of a countersuit? If so, it will get you nothing. I have no money, no job, no future. I can't even meet the costs of the trial."

"If you're looking for sympathy," said Calvin coldly, "don't look for it here. This was your doing. However, there will be no countersuit, neither of you nor of the university. We will even do what we can to keep you from going to prison for perjury. We aren't vindictive."

"Oh, is that why I'm not already in custody for forswearing myself? I had wondered. But then," he added bitterly, "why *should* you be vindictive? You have what you want now."

"Some of what we want, yes," said Calvin. "The university will keep Easy in its employ at a considerably higher rental fee. Furthermore, certain underground publicity concerning the trial will make it possible to place a few more of the EZ models in other institutions without danger of a repetition of this trouble."

"Then why have you come to see me?"

"Because I don't have all of what I want yet. I want to know why you hate robots as you do. Even if you had won the case, your reputation would have been ruined. The money you might have obtained could not have compensated for that. Would the satisfaction of your hatred for robots have done so?"

"Are you interested in *human* minds, Dr. Calvin?" asked Ninheimer, with acid mockery.

"Insofar as their reactions concern the welfare of robots, yes. For that reason, I have learned a little of human psychology."

"Enough of it to be able to trick me!"

"That wasn't hard," said Calvin, without pomposity. "The difficult thing was doing it in such a way as not to damage Easy."

"It is like you to be more concerned for a machine than for a man." He looked at her with savage contempt.

It left her unmoved. "It merely seems so, Professor Ninheimer. It is only by being concerned for robots that one can truly be concerned for twenty-first-century man. You would understand this if you were a roboticist."

"I have read enough robotics to know I don't *want* to be a roboticist!"

"Pardon me, you have read *a book* on robotics. It has taught you nothing. You learned enough to know that you could order a robot to do many things, even to falsify a book, if you went about it properly. You learned enough to know that you could not order him to forget something entirely without risking detection, but you thought you could order him into simple silence more safely. You were wrong."

"You guessed the truth from his silence?"

"It wasn't guessing. You were an amateur and didn't know enough to cover your tracks completely. My only problem was to prove the matter to the judge and you were kind enough to help us there, in your ignorance of the robotics you claim to despise."

"Is there any purpose in this discussion?" asked Ninheimer wearily.

"For me, yes," said Susan Calvin, "because I want you to understand how completely you have misjudged robots. You silenced Easy by telling him that if he told anyone about your own distortion of the book, you would lose your job. That set up a certain potential within Easy toward silence, one that was strong enough to resist our efforts to break it down. We would have damaged the brain if we had persisted.

"On the witness stand, however, you yourself put up a higher counterpotential. You said that because people would think that you, not a robot, had written the disputed passages in the book, you would lose far more than just your job. You would lose your reputation, your standing, your respect, your reason for living. You would lose the memory of you after death. A new and higher potential was set up by you—and Easy talked."

"Oh, God," said Ninheimer, turning his head away.

Calvin was inexorable. She said, "Do you understand *why* he talked? It was not to accuse you, but to *defend* you! It can be mathematically shown that he was about to assume full blame for your crime, to deny that you had anything to do with it. The First Law required that. He was going to lie—to damage himself—to bring monetary harm to a corporation. All that meant less to him than did the saving of you. If you really understood robots and robotics, you would have let him talk. But you did not understand, as I was sure you wouldn't, as I guaranteed to the defense attorney that you wouldn't. You were certain, in your hatred of robots, that Easy would act as a human being would act and defend itself at your expense. So you flared out at him in panic—and destroyed yourself."

Ninheimer said with feeling, "I hope some day your robots turn on you and kill you!"

"Don't be foolish," said Calvin. "Now I want you to explain why you've done all this."

Ninheimer grinned a distorted, humorless grin. "I am to dissect my mind, am I, for your intellectual curiosity, in return for immunity from a charge of perjury?"

"Put it that way if you like," said Calvin emotionlessly. "But explain."

"So that you can counter future anti-robot attempts more efficiently? With greater understanding?"

"I accept that."

"You know," said Ninheimer, "I'll tell you—just to watch it do you no good at all. You can't understand human motivation. You can only understand your damned machines because you're a machine yourself, with skin on."

He was breathing hard and there was no hesitation in his speech, no searching for precision. It was as though he had no further use for precision.

He said, "For two hundred and fifty years, the machine has been replacing Man and destroying the handcraftsman. Pottery is spewed out of molds and presses. Works of art have been replaced by identical gimcracks stamped out on a die. Call it progress, if you wish! The artist is restricted to abstractions, confined to the world of ideas. He must design something in mind—and then the machine does the rest.

"Do you suppose the potter is content with mental creation? Do you suppose the idea is enough? That there is nothing in the feel of the clay itself, in watching the thing grow as hand and mind work *together?* Do you suppose the actual growth doesn't act as a feedback to modify and improve the idea?"

"You are not a potter," said Dr. Calvin.

"I am a creative artist! I design and build articles and books. There is more to it than the mere thinking of words and of putting them in the right order. If that were all, there would be no pleasure in it, no return.

"A book should take shape in the hands of the writer. One must actually see the chapters grow and develop. One must work and rework and watch the changes take place beyond the original concept even. There is taking the galleys in hand and seeing how the sentences look in print and molding them again. There are a hundred contacts between a man and his work at every stage of the game—and the contact itself is pleasurable and repays a man for the work he puts into his creation more than anything else could. *Your robot would take all that away.*"

"So does a typewriter. So does a printing press. Do you propose to return to the hand illumination of manuscripts?"

"Typewriters and printing presses take away some, but your robot would deprive us of all. Your robot takes over the galleys. Soon it, or other robots, would take over the original writing, the searching of the sources, the checking and cross-checking of passages, perhaps even the deduction of conclusions. What would that leave the scholar? One thing only—the barren decisions concerning what orders to give the robot next! I want to save the future generations of the world of scholarship from such a final hell. That meant more to me than even my own reputation and so I set out to destroy U.S. Robots by whatever means."

"You were bound to fail," said Susan Calvin.

"I was bound to try," said Simon Ninheimer.

Calvin turned and left. She did her best to feel no pang of sympathy for the broken man.

She did not entirely succeed.

137